# SPYNOSAUR

## VS GOLDENCLAW

STRIPES PUBLISHING LIMITED
An imprint of the Little Tiger Group
1 Coda Studios, 189 Munster Road, London SW6 6AW

Imported into the EEA by Penguin Random House Ireland,
Morrison Chambers, 32 Nassau Street, Dublin D02 YH68

A paperback original
First published in Great Britain in 2017

Text copyright © Guy Bass, 2017
Illustrations copyright © Lee Robinson, 2017

ISBN: 978-1-84715-778-2

A CIP catalogue record for this book is available from the
British Library.

Printed and bound in the UK.

MIX
Paper from
responsible sources
FSC® C020471

The Forest Stewardship Council® (FSC®) is a global, not-for-
profit organization dedicated to the promotion of responsible
forest management worldwide. FSC defines standards based on
agreed principles for responsible forest stewardship that are
supported by environmental, social, and economic stakeholders.
To learn more, visit www.fsc.org

10 9 8 7 6 5 4 3 2

# SPYNOSAUR

## VS GOLDENCLAW

ILLUSTRATED BY
# GUY BASS    LEE ROBINSON

To Ian
Thanks for keeping me in coffee and crisps.
– Guy Bass

For my favourite artist, Amanda.
– Lee Robinson

LITTLE TIGER
LONDON

When top *spy*-entists put the mind of super-spy Agent Gambit inside the body of a dinosaur, they created the first ever **Super Secret Agent Dinosaur.** Together with his daughter, Amber, this prehistoric hero protects the world from villainy.

His code name:

# SPYNOSAUR

**FROM A LAND BEFORE TIME COMES A HERO FOR TODAY...**

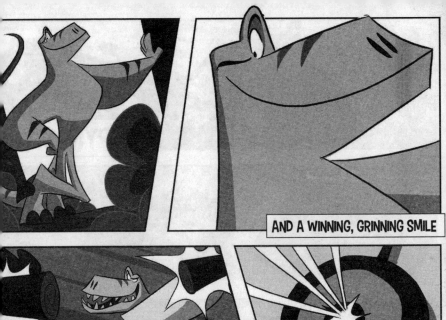

AND A WINNING, GRINNING SMILE

HE'S THE DARING DAPPER DINO
WITH THE PREHISTORIC STYLE!

HE'S THE SCALED 'N' TAILED AGENT WHO IS CERTAIN TO SURPRISE

BUT HE STILL LOOKS LIKE A DINOSAUR, WHATEVER HIS DISGUISE

SPYNOSAUR!

# 1.
# DIVA FEVER

"THE PRIMA DONNA" AIRSHIP,
FLYING HIGH ABOVE THE VILLAGE
OF LITTLE WALLOP, ENGLAND

"Everything is going according to – Aatchoo! – plan!" said Diva Fever, blowing her permanently blocked nose in front of her assembled henchmen. She flounced up and down the airship's long, teardrop-shaped control centre, making sure the light pouring through its many windows made her sequined dress glitter and sparkle. "Once I activate my under-the-weather weapon, the citizens of this sleepy village are – Aatchoo! – *doobed*!"

DEPARTMENT 6

CLASSIFILE                    #M4R14H

CODE NAME: DIVA FEVER

>> World-famous singer whose
career was cut short by an
incurable cold. Subject has
since turned to a life of
crime - she is obsessed with
inflicting her victims with a
case of the sniffles.

DEPARTMENT 6

"The Common Cold Cannon is fully charged and ready to fire, Your Diva-ness," grunted one of the henchmen from a console at the front of the airship's control centre.

"Doobed, I say!" continued Diva Fever. "Doobed to having a slight temperature ... doobed to having to blow their doses ... doobed to feeling off-colour for an entire week!"

"Hardly the crime of the century," sighed one of the henchmen loudly.

"Who — Aatchoo! — said that?" hissed Diva Fever, glowering at her four henchmen in turn.

They all had shaved heads and were dressed in drab, grey jumpsuits, with small black masks covering their eyes. They looked almost identical ... except for one.

One of them looked a *lot* like a dinosaur.

The scaly "henchman" towered over the other lackeys and a long, green tail poked out from his jumpsuit. He adjusted his mask, yellow lizard eyes glinting.

"You! The newbie!" Diva Fever growled, oblivious to her so-called henchman's true identity. "Did you dare insult by diabolical – Aatchoo! – plot?"

"You call giving a few people a touch of the flu 'diabolical'?" replied the disguised dinosaur.

"How dare you doubt by evil plans! I have a good bind to fling you out of the airship by your tail!" Diva snapped. "Wait ... *tail*?"

"Surprise," said the dinosaur. With a swing of that great tail he sent Diva Fever flying. The henchmen scattered in horror as the dinosaur tore off his tiny mask.

"Sp-Spynosaur! The super secret agent dinosaur!" cried a horrified henchman.

"He must not foil by plan! Hold hib off! I'll fire the Cobbon Cold Cannon!" howled Diva Fever, leaping to her feet.

Spynosaur let out a loud sigh, before diving at the hapless henchmen in a blur of movement.

In moments, the henchmen lay unconscious in a pile. But they had given Diva Fever just enough time to reach the cannon's console. As she reached for the FIRE button, Spynosaur drew a grapple-gun from his henchman outfit and took aim. One shot and his grappling hook would streak forth, hooking his foe and putting an end to her scheme. One shot...

"Oh, what's the point?" Spynosaur mumbled to himself and lowered his gun.

"The village is doobed!" cried Diva Fever, a semi-split-second from pressing FIRE. "Doo—"

# "AMBITIOUS SPINNING CRAZY~ GOLF SEA~TURTLE KICK!"

## THWUMP!

The last thing Diva Fever saw was the air above her head shimmer as an almost-invisible figure leaped towards her.

"That little wallop is for messing with Little Wallop!" declared the disembodied voice. As Diva Fever crumpled to the floor, the air shimmered again and Spynosaur's daughter and sidekick, Amber, appeared. She was a girl of ten, with bright copper hair and a face full of freckles.

"This *stealth-suit* is officially awesome," Amber added, inspecting her sleek, grey jumpsuit. "Being almost invisible while ninja-kicking villains is my new favourite thing! Also, cartoons."

DEPARTMENT 6 ●○✕≡

**CLASSIFILE** #S-M-L-XL-XXL

CODE NAME: **"SLY SPY"**
**STEALTH-SUIT**

>> Hi-tech spy-suit,
capable of rendering the
wearer almost invisible
for short periods of
time. Machine washable.

DEPARTMENT 6

Spynosaur tossed Diva Fever on to the pile of henchmen. From his jumpsuit he produced a small, metal sphere and threw it at the vanquished villains... A second later the sphere exploded, releasing a huge, transparent bubble that engulfed Diva and her henchmen entirely. Spynosaur slid open the airship's door and rolled the felon-filled sphere towards it.

"Now it's time for your *pun*-ishment…" Amber declared.

Spynosaur opened his mouth as if to speak, but after a moment he just shrugged … and then booted the bubble out into mid-air.

"AAAAAAA-tchoo!" screamed Diva Fever as she and her henchmen plunged towards the ground.

"Wait, no puns? You *always* do puns!" cried Amber. She hung out of the airship and shouted after the plummeting bubble. "That'll teach you to be *sniffy*! Sorry to give you the *cold* shoulder! *Snot* looking so good for you now!" Amber turned to her dad. "Uh, weren't we meant to take Diva back to Department 6?"

"What's the point?" Spynosaur replied with a sigh. "It's not like she's diabolical enough to do any harm … not really."

Amber scratched her head.

"Well, can we at least blow the airship to smithereens?" she asked hopefully.

"Why not just let it float away?" Spynosaur said wistfully. "Float away, like lost dreams..."

"But we *always* blow up something," Amber replied.

Spynosaur just stared up into the sky, looking oddly lost. "Float away, float away, lost to the skies," he began. "When the villains are gone, what use are we spies?"

"Da-ad, not another *poem* ... I keep telling you, spying and poetry don't mix!" Amber groaned.

## 2.
# A LIFE WITHOUT SPYING

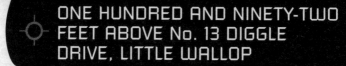

ONE HUNDRED AND NINETY-TWO
FEET ABOVE No. 13 DIGGLE
DRIVE, LITTLE WALLOP

Spynosaur opened his parachute much earlier than normal (he usually waited until the last possible moment to keep things death-defying), so he and Amber had a leisurely descent towards Little Wallop, which, by chance, was where Amber lived with her mum.

"Are you all right, Dad?" Amber asked as they floated towards her house. "That's the third time this week you've *not* blown something up... It's been so long since you made a pun I've started doing it for you... And the *poetry*? Don't even get me started on the poetry..."

"Sorry ... I guess my heart's not in it," Spynosaur sighed. "It's been *months* since we captured the P.O.I.S.O.N. high command. Since then, no one's come close to filling their diabolical boots. All that's left are novelty villains – Diva Fever .... Brad Grammar and the Split Infinitives ... The Tickle Monster... What I wouldn't give for a real nemesis – a diabolical criminal mastermind worthy of my astonishingly impressive spy skills."

"But isn't stopping all the villains the point of being a spy?" asked Amber.

"But what's the point of a spy without villains?" Spynosaur replied. "Without them, I'm just a man trapped in the body of a dinosaur ... and dinosaurs belong in the past."

Amber's blood ran cold – her dad sounded like he was losing the will to spy! What if he decided to give it up altogether? As far as Amber was concerned, a life without spying was no life at all...

AMBER'S LIFE BEFORE SPYING

Spynosaur and Amber landed on the front lawn of number 13 Diggle Drive just as Amber's mum stepped out of the front door carrying a bin bag. They quickly leaped behind a wheelie bin. Amber's mum had no idea about Amber's secret life as Spynosaur's sidekick — as far as she was concerned, Amber was just like any other ten-year-old and her dad had been a simple peanut-butter salesman who met his end in a tragic kite-flying accident. Spies and secret-keeping went hand in hand.

"Amber! Are you out here? Breakfast's ready," called Amber's mum. "Where's that girl got to?"

Amber glanced at her dad, who had somehow contorted his massive body in such a way as to hide himself behind a single wheelie bin. Amber dared not move a muscle, even to activate her *stealth-suit*'s almost invisibility. She held her breath as she heard her mum lift the bin lid...

"Amber! There you are!" said Amber's mum.

Amber was sure she'd been spotted. She was about to look up when:

"Yes, I am here, my mother," said a deep, gruff voice. Amber dared to peek round the bin. Behind her mum stood a short, old man with a face like cracked stone. He wore a red wig not unlike Amber's own hair.

"I was playing in garden with hula-hula-hoop, like normal child of my age," continued Sergei. "Now I will be eating breakfast."

CLASSIFILE    #1984-1-CCCP

CODE NAME: SERGEI
AKA AGENT A64

>> Undercover agent and semi-
retired master of disguise.
Subject acts as a double
for Agent Amber when she
accompanies Spynosaur on
missions. (SEE: SPYNOSAUR)

DEPARTMENT
6

"I hope you're hungry," said Amber's mum, dropping the bag into the bin and making her way back to the house. "I've made your favourite!"

"Boiled pig's heart in salt jelly?" Sergei said hopefully.

"No, silly, Scrambled Egg Surprise!" laughed Amber's mum. Sergei grumbled loudly and followed her back inside.

"Yes!" Amber cried, leaping to her feet. She was about to rush into the house and relieve Sergei of his breakfast-eating duties when she spotted her dad, still contorted behind the dustbin and looking oddly lost. "Uh, are you going to be OK, Dad? I mean, I could stay with you, if—"

"And have you miss Scrambled Egg Surprise?" Spynosaur replied with a smile. "No, you go in — I'll see you when the world needs saving ag—"

# BA-DEEP!
# BA-DEEP!
# BA-DEEP!

Spynosaur and Amber checked their Super Secret Spy Watches™.

"The signal!" Amber whispered excitedly. "We're needed!"

"Probably a cat stuck up a tree or something equally un-diabolical," huffed Spynosaur. He tapped his watch with a clawed finger to summon the Dino-soarer.

DEPARTMENT 6
CLASSIFILE    #1984-DZ-DB8

CODE NAME:
THE DINO-SOARER
>> Supersonic saurian-styled
stealth jet. Specially adapted
for pilots with tails. Equipped
with invisibility mode, gravity
beam, missile launchers, front
and rear laser cannons and
built-in Wi-Fi.

DEPARTMENT
6

Amber saw the leaves of the trees shake as her dad's almost-invisible jet-plane descended through the sky towards them.

"Or *maybe* it's a brand-new criminal mastermind for us to defeat!" Amber said, trying to sound positive. "Eggs can wait... Let's go!"

# 3.
# THE RAY EMITTER
## AKA RONALD RAY-GUN

DEPARTMENT 6 HEADQUARTERS,
BENEATH THE NATURAL HISTORY
MUSEUM OF LONDON, LONDON.

Before long, Spynosaur and Amber had arrived in London. The Dino-soarer landed invisibly atop the Natural History Museum and deposited the agents down a chimney. With a **FWOOOOMP** they hurtled through long, metallic tubes and into Department 6's underground headquarters.

The control room was filled with banks of computers and machinery and smelled of vanilla air freshener. No sooner had Spynosaur and Amber emerged than they were confronted by a distractingly tall man with large glasses and an explosion of unkempt hair.

"Spynosaur! You're just in time!" Dr Newfangle hollered. Spynosaur let out a dispirited grunt.

"We came at supersonic speed!" said Amber. "Where's M11? What's the mission?"

"Mission? I haven't the foggiest ... I meant you're just in time for today's *spy-ence rap*!" Newfangle replied excitedly. "It's all about my greatest invention, the Variable Super Science Ray Beam Emitter!" He pressed a button by the door and the wall slid aside to reveal a brightly lit stage. In the centre stood a huge machine, comprised of a large silver dome atop three long legs that looked like a giant camera tripod. On one side of the dome was a round dial and on the other, an impressive barrel.

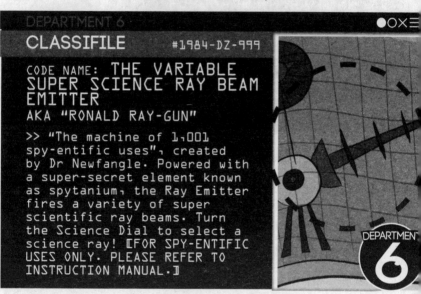

DEPARTMENT 6 ●○X≡

**CLASSIFILE**   #1984-DZ-999

CODE NAME: **THE VARIABLE SUPER SCIENCE RAY BEAM EMITTER**
AKA "RONALD RAY-GUN"

>> "The machine of 1,001 spy-entific uses", created by Dr Newfangle. Powered with a super-secret element known as spytanium, the Ray Emitter fires a variety of super scientific ray beams. Turn the Science Dial to select a science ray! [FOR SPY-ENTIFIC USES ONLY. PLEASE REFER TO INSTRUCTION MANUAL.]

DEPARTMENT **6**

"We don't have time for 'Ronald Ray-Gun' now," said Amber. "Where's—"

"Give me a phat beat!" interrupted Newfangle excitedly. He produced a microphone from his lab coat and hopped on to the stage with the Ray Emitter. And so began:

# DR NEWFANGLE'S SUPER SPY-ENCE RAP

**Reduction Ray!** You can shrink a car
And put it in your pocket
'til you need to go far
**Gravity Ray!** Yo, here's an education
Increase or decrease it
to suit your situation
Turn the **Science Dial** like you be rollin' a dice
Then switch to **Groundhog Ray**
so you can make it happen twice
Evolving, transforming, transfiguring galore!
We got **rays for days** and
there ain't no one keeping score
**Fifty Shades of Ray!** Or maybe even more
It's even got a ray
to grow a **spying dinosaur!**

"That reminds me of a poem I just wrote," said Spynosaur, staring into the distance. "I call it 'Topography of Sadness (Where Are All The Villains?)', and it goes something like—"

"Seriously! Where's M11?" Amber yelled in desperation. "We've got a mission to—"

"Holey Moley!" Newfangle cried.

"What? What is it?" Amber replied.

"No, *Holey Moley* is our new Head of Security. He too is a product of science rays," explained Newfangle. "Look, here he comes now..."

"But what about the— Eep!" Amber said, almost treading on the tiny, spy-suit-wearing mole that scurried between her legs and across the floor towards the Ray Emitter.

"A mole in Department 6?" Amber mused, inspecting the tiny creature. He was only a few centimetres long, with black fur and a twitching, pink snout.

## CLASSIFILE     #WITW-1908

CODE NAME: HOLEY MOLEY
AKA AGENT A64

>> Following a disastrous mission
involving a swarm of robotic
killer bees and forty-two gallons
of honey, the mind of agent A64
was transferred into the body of
a spy-entifically modified mole,
created by Newfangle's Science
Rays. [SEE: DR NEWFANGLE, ERGO
EGO.]

DEPARTMENT **6**

"Holey Moley, be so kind as to return my excellent invention to the Department Vault with my other excellent inventions," ordered Newfangle.

"Not a problem! Leave it to me! I can – *gnngh* – do it!" Holey Moley replied, pushing the Ray Emitter with all his mole-might, edging it millimetre by millimetre across the floor. "Look, I'm helping! Please don't – *gnngh!* – fire me..."

"Is – is he OK?" Amber said to her dad.

"Course he's not OK, he's a blinkin' mole!" said a voice. A monkey in a grey spy-suit came screeching towards them, riding one of Newfangle's *spycycle* jet-bikes.

CLASSIFILE #2-MALPA

CODE NAME: DANGER MONKEY
AKA AGENT A41

>> Following an unfortunate
incident involving a punctured
parachute and a pool of
piranhas, Agent A41's mind
was transferred into a
spy-entifically modified
spider-monkey, created by
Dr Newfangle's Science Rays.
Quick to anger. Would rather
have been turned into a
dinosaur.

DEPARTMENT 6

"Moley 'ere's got a cripplin' inferiority complex on account of his diminutive stature," added Danger Monkey, hopping down from the spycycle as an exhausted Holey Moley edged the Ray Emitter slowly across the room. "D'you know 'ow 'ard it is t' get anythin' done when yer a mole? Or a monkey for that matter? Maybe if Newfangle had put our brainwaves into somethin' useful like a *dinosaur* ... I mean, you don't see no one treadin' on ol' Spyno 'ere!"

"The day's not over yet," hissed a voice. M11 strode out of her office at the other end of the room, her imposing moustache twitching impatiently. The head of Department 6 glowered at Spynosaur and folded her arms. "And if anyone's going to put the *boot* into Spynosaur, it's me."

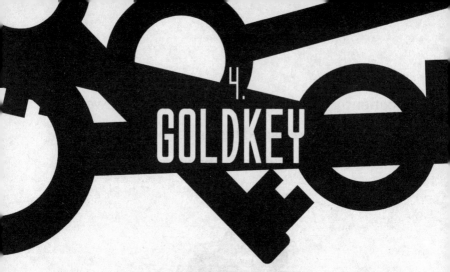

# 4.
# GOLDKEY

"Better late than never, Spynosaur – although where you're concerned, I'd prefer *never*," M11 said, eyeballing the saurian secret agent. "You're a maddening maverick whose routine recklessness belongs in the past ... just like dinosaurs!"

DEPARTMENT 6

CLASSIFILE          #1984-DZ-M11

Code Name: M11
(Formerly known as A12)

>> Head of Department 6.
As straight-laced as
straight lace, with a
no-nonsense approach to
nonsense and a hard-nosed
approach to noses. Lives by,
and occasionally cuddles,
the rulebook. Hobbies
include well kept moustaches
and shouting.

DEPARTMENT
6

Amber winced. She was relieved M11 still thought Spynosaur was a "maddening maverick" but it was only a matter of time before she found out that he'd lost his will to spy.

*We'd be fired on the spot!* Amber thought. *Thrown out of Department 6!*

"So, where's Diva Fever?" M11 continued. "*Please* don't tell me you blew her to smithereens..."

Spynosaur glazed over and replied:

"Why blow things to smithereens,

When all we have are broken dreams.

The world is safe, no need to spy,

Perhaps it's time to say goodb—"

"We blew up loads! Boom! Smashooh! Ka-splosion!" interrupted a desperate Amber. "So what's our next mission? It's a diabolical new villain trying to take over the world, right? Right?"

"I'll get on to the mission when I'm good and ready! So, on to the mission," M11 said. "Pay attention, agents – I don't like repeating myself. Now, pay attention, agents! Your mission is to transport our four most diabolical criminals from our maximum-security prison here at Department 6 headquarters to a new maximum-security facility just down the road."

"Move P.O.I.S.O.N.? What's the point?" Spynosaur asked. "It's not like they're causing us any trouble here, more's the pity..."

"Blast it to smithereens, Spynosaur, this is a secret agency, not a debating society!" growled M11. "I have decided that the heads of P.O.I.S.O.N. should now be detained by a security firm known as *Goldkey*©. Agents, your mission is to accompany the prisoners in Goldkey©'s armoured transporter to the Goldkey© Prison. Goldkey© will be providing a team of armed guards as backup."

"Backup?" Danger Monkey scoffed. "We don't need no 'and-'olding from a bunch o' chumps!"

"Neither I, nor my therapist, give a monkey's what you think, Danger Monkey. Just stick to the plan!" snapped M11. She reached into her pocket and took out a piece of folded-up paper. "Speaking of which, here it is..."

"I'll only say this once — get out there and do your job," concluded M11. "Now get out there and do your job!"

# 5.
# ATTACK OF THE HENCHMEN

THE STREETS OF LONDON,
THE CITY OF LONDON, LONDON

Danger Monkey drove the huge Goldkey© transporter down the London streets. Inside, a dozen Goldkey© guards accompanied Spynosaur and Amber. They were identically clad in crisp, black uniforms, with a large golden key emblazoned on their chests. Their belts were laden with electrified batter-batons and exploding handcuffs. Only the Goldkey© chief's bright orange beard made him stand out from his team. He stood guard over the four criminal masterminds, each trapped within their own cell:

FANDANGO SCARAMOOSH
Flamboyant Fiend

GUMS GAMBINO
Mouthy Mobster

SHADY LADY
Mistress of Menace

ERGO EGO
Insidious Inventor

As Spynosaur brooded in the corner of the transporter, Amber paced up and down the cages that lined one side of the long trailer, eyeballing the villains in turn.

"Not so tough now, eh?" she mocked, waggling her finger at them. "Not without your henchmen and your secret weapons and your doomsday devices and your evil schemes and your—"

"Don't mock the villains, Amber, there's a good girl," her dad said.

"But — but we *always* mock the villains," Amber huffed.

"Spynosaur, isn't it plain I'm not part of this P.O.I.S.O.N.-ous pack? My undoubted devotion ... is to you," cooed Shady Lady. The lean, black-clad villain was permanently shrouded in shadow, even in her brightly lit cell. "Who could devise a more delicious duo? The femme fatale and her prehistoric pugilist! We could be immortalized in infamy..."

"What in the name of my tailor's tape measure are you saying, Shady?" howled Fandango Scaramoosh, flicking his huge quiff of silvery hair. "Are you attempting to *woo* our arch-nemesis?"

"Yeah, what's the big idea, tryin' to distance yerself from our disreputable undertakin's?" grunted Gums Gambino, his large, flapping lips sending saliva flying through the bars of his cell. "You reckon you can bat your eyelids at dat dumb dino and he'll let you go?"

"Spynosaur's a stupid head!" added the egg-headed Ergo Ego.

"What can I say? I'm drawn to danger ... and nothing is more *dangerous* than a dinosaur," said Shady Lady, blowing Spynosaur a kiss.

"Eww!" howled Amber.

"*None* of you are getting out..." Spynosaur sighed disappointedly. "You're all going to rot in jail for the rest of your—"

The transporter lurched, throwing Spynosaur, Amber and the Goldkey© guards through the air. A second later, they felt the transporter rock and roll on to its side.

"What was *that*?" cried Amber, scrambling to her feet.

"We're under attack!" howled Danger Monkey. "Someone's tryin' t' make a monkey out of us!"

"Probably just a burst tyre," huffed Spynosaur. He clambered to the back door. "Amber, stay here and keep an eye on the prisoners, will you?"

Spynosaur swung the door open and climbed out on to the busy London street, tall buildings looming on either side. Cars swerved to avoid the chaos (and the sight of a real live dinosaur) as plumes of smoke billowed from the transporter. Danger Monkey was right — they'd been hit! A massive impact had blown the transporter on to its side. Spynosaur glanced back up the road.

A man in a black-and-white maid's outfit stood in the middle of the street, holding a bazooka.

"A *Maid Man* – one of Gums Gambino's personal henchmen," said Spynosaur. "But how could he know about—?"

"Spyno, we've got company!" cried Danger Monkey, clambering out of the transporter's cab. He pointed up the road as more figures emerged from the smoke – twenty at least – armed to the teeth and closing in fast.

"It's an 'ole 'enchmen army!" Danger Monkey howled. "Where do P.O.I.S.O.N. find all these do-no-good dummies?"

Gums Gambino's frilly-aproned Maid Men led the charge, flanked on one side by Ergo Ego's Egotists, dressed in egg-shaped suits of armour, while on the other, Fandango Scaramoosh's flamboyant Fine 'n' Dandies, each clad in a colour

47

of the rainbow, danced towards them. And leaping in and out of the shadows of cars, buildings and passers-by, the spectral figures of Shady Lady's un-deadly Friends Fatale closed in on the transporter.

"There's too many of 'em!" said Danger Monkey, jumping down from the transporter. "We're outnumbered and outgunned! We don't stand a chance!"

Spynosaur tapped the timer on his Super Secret Spy Watch™ ... and, for the first time in months, a sharp-toothed grin spread across his face.

"And about time, too," he said.

# 6. DOUBLE CROSS!

"Thirty-seven seconds ... I'm out of practice," Spynosaur said, checking his Super Secret Spy Watch™. The henchmen horde lay sprawled across the street. "Still, that was almost *too* easy..."

"Easy for you to say 'easy'..." groaned Danger Monkey, crawling out from underneath the limp body of a henchman. He had clumps of hair missing from his hide and a smouldering tail. "I ain't built for this sort of – *oww* – monkey business."

"My spy super senses are never wrong – and they're telling me something's not right," Spynosaur said, dusting himself off. "How did the henchmen know we were moving the prisoners, unless somebody tipped them off? The only other people who knew about it were—"

**KRUMP!** Spynosaur didn't even see the Goldkey© batter-baton coming. It struck him hard on the jaw; he stumbled back, a sharp tooth flying from his mouth, and fell to the ground.

"Dad!" came a cry. A dazed Spynosaur looked up and saw his daughter with the Goldkey© chief's elbow hooked round her neck. The chief's electrified batter-baton sparked next to Amber's face.

"Sorry, Dad," Amber replied, as more Goldkey© guards closed in. "This beardy stinker grabbed me before I could put my epic ninja moves on him."

"Drop your weapons, agents, or the sidekick gets it!" ordered the chief. "And by 'it' I mean a nasty case of electrocution."

"Security guards, my eye ... you're just more *henchmen*," Spynosaur said, getting to his feet. He snarled, exposing the gap where his tooth had been. Then he drew his pistol and threw it to the ground.

"No good traitors t' Queen an' country!" howled Danger Monkey, pulling a banana from his shoulder-holster and tossing it away. "I'll bite yer toenails! I'll pluck yer nose 'air! I'll break into yer place of work and eat yer packed lunch!"

"Fit them with Goldie-locks©," ordered the chief. The Goldkey© henchmen quickly bound their wrists with hi-tech golden handcuffs. "If you so much as *twitch*, those handcuffs will explode," the beacon-bearded chief continued. "There'll be nothing left of you except dino-DNA..."

"But I need to scratch me nose!" declared

Danger Monkey, inspecting his handcuffs. "All this dust and smoke is aggravatin' me allergies..."

"Dad...?" muttered Amber, hoping he had some sort of plan.

"It's all right, Amber. We'll let them play their hand..." began Spynosaur. As if on cue, two Goldkey© henchmen helped Shady Lady out of the transporter. She was free.

"Shady Lady! What about the rest of us?" howled Ergo Ego from inside his cell. "Don't leave us locked up in here, you stupid—!"

The Goldkey© henchmen slammed the transporter door shut.

"So sorry, it seems my saviours want me solo," said Shady Lady.

"Shady! This was all your doin'!" Danger Monkey cried. "All them 'enchmen was just a distraction, keepin' Spyno busy while you made yer escape!"

"And yet, she's more surprised than anyone to be free – aren't you, Shady Lady?" Spynosaur added, fixing his saurian stare upon the villainess. "Someone *else* is behind all this ... but who? Who would go to all this trouble just to free you?"

"Jealous, my prehistoric paragon?" said Shady Lady, bending down to pluck Spynosaur's tooth from the ground. She turned it in her slender fingers and examined it closely. "I'll always have a soft spot for you, Spynosaur, but it seems I'm due a date with Destiny. *Adieu*, agent."

"You're not going anywhere!" said Amber, the Goldkey© chief's batter-baton crackling next to her face. "This is London – the traffic's a *nightmare*."

"If the roads are busy, take the Underground!"

the chief replied with a smirk.

Suddenly a low, ground-shaking rumble filled the air and the road beneath them exploded with a **KROOOOOM!** Tarmac flew in every direction as a huge, golden drill burst, spinning, from the ground. In less than a second, a vast subterranean tank emerged, clad entirely in gold, its still-whirring drill-bit gleaming in the midday sun.

"We call it the Gold Digger!" the chief added as a door of the tank opened and a motorized ramp slid out from inside. "After you, Shady Lady."

"A marvellous means of making off," noted Shady Lady. She disappeared inside, followed by the Goldkey© henchmen. The chief was halfway up the ramp before he turned back and flung Amber to the ground.

"Amber!" cried the cuffed Spynosaur, unable to move as the ramp withdrew and the door closed. A moment later, the Gold Digger burrowed into the ground. In a whirring gold flash, it vanished into darkness.

"Yeah, you'd better run!" cried Amber, her voice echoing down the tunnel as the rumble of the Gold Digger began to fade. She scrambled to her feet and turned back to her dad and Danger Monkey, frozen to the spot, their explosive-laden handcuffs locked round their wrists.

"Uh, Spyno? We might 'ave a problem ... I mean, *another* problem," Danger Monkey noted, his nose twitching uncontrollably. "If I don't scratch my nose in the next two seconds, I'm going to aa-Aa-AAA—"

"Amber, into the tunnel, now!" roared Spynosaur.

"But—" began Amber.

"**NOW!**" Spynosaur roared.

Amber spun on her heel and dived into the tunnel, just as Danger Monkey let out an almighty sneeze.

"AAAtch—"

# 7.
# STOLEN SCIENCE

IT'S LOOKING PRETTY LIKELY
THAT OUR HERO LOST THE FIGHT.
"BOOM!" WENT THE EXPLOSION –
THERE'S NO WAY THAT HE'S ALL RIGHT!
WITH A SNEEZE THAT BOMB EXPLODED,
IT WENT OFF BEFORE OUR EYES.
SO I GUESS THE STORY'S OVER,
HOW COULD ANYONE SURVIVE?

# SPYNOSAUR...?

"Dad...?" groaned Amber as she dragged herself out of the tunnel, her ears still ringing from the explosion. She was faced with a blinding wall of thick smoke. "Dad! No, you can't be—"

"Reports of my death have been *blown* out of proportion," said a voice as the smoke cleared. Amber looked up to see Spynosaur, cradling a singed and stunned Danger Monkey.

"A pun ... an actual, terrible pun!" cried Amber. "I never thought I'd be so glad to hear— Wait, how did you survive the explosion? How did you get out of the cuffs? How are you not *dead*?"

"There's a simple explanation," began Spynosaur. "You see—"

## SPYNOSAUR!
## COME IN, SPYNOSAUR!

"The Department 6 ... super top secret ... transmission channel," wheezed Danger Monkey, smoke puffing from his mouth.

Spynosaur tapped a button on his Super Secret Spy Watch™.

"You can stop worrying, M11, it's good news," he said, giving Amber a wink. "I'm alive and well and feeling better than ever!"

"You and I have very different opinions on what constitutes 'good news', Spynosaur," huffed M11 through Spynosaur's watch. "What's going on there? I heard the explosions all the way from HQ! Don't tell me the unthinkable has happened..."

"Sheep 'ave started doin' ballet?" said Danger Monkey.

"I'm talking about P.O.I.S.O.N.!" M11 barked. "Do you still have them all under lock and key?"

"All except one," Spynosaur admitted. "Goldkey© set us up — it was all an elaborate plan to free Shady Lady."

"Blast it to smithereens, that's not possible!"

cried M11. "I cleared Goldkey© for top-secret duty myself!"

"We've got bigger problems!" Newfangle's panicked voice blared over Spynosaur's Super Secret Spy Watch™.

"Newfangle, what are you doing in my office?" snapped M11. "You know I don't like to be interrupted when I'm shouting at Spynosaur..."

"But the unthinkable has happened!" insisted Newfangle.

"All cheese has turned invisible?" said Danger Monkey.

"Someone's broken into the Vault!" Newfangle cried. "All of my most excellent inventions are in there!"

"We'll be there in five minutes," said Spynosaur. Then he looked at Amber, a grin spreading across his face. "A break-in, eh? The plot thickens ... and about time, too."

## THE VAULT, DEPARTMENT 6 HEADQUARTERS

Spynosaur, Amber, M11, Danger Monkey and a flustered Newfangle gathered in the middle of the Vault. The vast, impenetrable metal cube housed the Department's most impressive technology – Newfangle's inventions lined every wall, from a pair of jet-powered spycycles to a rack of imploding pullovers to a bazooka-firing bazooka.

But today the Vault looked notably different. In the middle of the floor was a huge hole. It was as if the ground had exploded.

"It looks just like the tunnel the Gold Digger made!" noted Amber, peering into the tunnel.

"Well spotted, Amber," replied Spynosaur. "This case just took on a *hole* new dimension. But what were they looking—"

"NOOooooOOoo!" cried Newfangle, falling to his knees. "The unthinkable has happened!"

"Knitting's been made illegal?" said Danger Monkey.

"The Variable Super Science Ray Beam Emitter has been stolen!" howled Newfangle. "Look!"

Sure enough, a sign on the wall read VARIABLE SUPER SCIENCE RAY BEAM EMITTER ... but beneath it there was only a Ray Emitter-sized space where once stood Newfangle's greatest invention.

"Those double-crossers must 'ave 'it the Vaults

at the same time we were busy scrappin'! They was after Ronald Ray-Gun!" growled Danger Monkey, wrapping bandages round his various burns and breaks.

"This is a nightmare!" Newfangle howled. He checked his watch. "No, a *daymare*! With the power of the Variable Super Science Ray Beam Emitter, an enemy could form, fashion, transmute or transmogrify whatever they pleased – even a dinosaur!"

"Now that sounds like an enemy I could really get my *teeth* into," said Spynosaur with a grin. Amber hoped that was *exactly* what was going to happen – surely nothing would guarantee her dad's happiness (and career in spying) more than taking on some sort of deadly dino-double!

"One prehistoric pain in the neck is more than enough, thank you very much!" M11 snapped. "Ronald Ray-Gun must be retrieved!"

"'Ang on a sec," said Danger Monkey. "'Ow did they take Ronald Ray-Gun without setting off the alarm? The only way to turn it off is from *inside* the Vault."

"Good point, Danger Monkey," said Spynosaur. "How *alarming* ... it appears the Department has a mole."

"You don't mean ... you can't mean ... actually, what do you mean?" asked M11.

"I mean, we have in our midst the only kind of agent I cannot stand," explained Spynosaur. "A *double* agent."

# 8.
# THE MOLE AND THE RED HERRING

"A double agent in the Department? Let me at 'em!" snarled Danger Monkey. "I'll teach 'em to be traitorous! I'll blunt their pencils!"

"We need to find out who was in the Vault when the alarm was deactivated," said Spynosaur.

"Holey Moley!" cried Dr Newfangle.

"What? What is it?" Amber asked.

"No, I mean it was Holey Moley who returned the Variable Super Science Ray Beam Emitter to the Vault," Newfangle explained. "He must have turned off the alarm when he was down here. He must be the mole!"

"Did someone ask for the Head of Security? Agent Moley, reporting for duty!" said Holey Moley, scurrying, as if on cue, inside the Vault. "What happened down here? Can I help? I can help!"

"You can 'elp by confessin', mole!" howled Danger Monkey, picking up Holey Moley by the scruff of his neck and dangling him in the air. "You turned off the alarm, admit it! Admit yer the mole!"

"M-mole? Not me!" replied Holey Moley. "I mean, obviously I'm a mole, but—"

"So it was you!" Amber cried.

"No, I didn't turn off anything! I can prove it!" squeaked Holey Moley. With more than a little embarrassment, he added, "I-I didn't have the strength to get Ronald Ray-Gun back to the Vault on my own, so I asked another agent to help me with it..."

"Another agent? Who?" snapped M11.

"Her, who!" replied Holey Moley, pointing at the Vault doorway. A motorized platform rolled into the Vault, atop which sat a fishbowl filled with water. Inside the bowl was a small, scarlet-scaled herring.

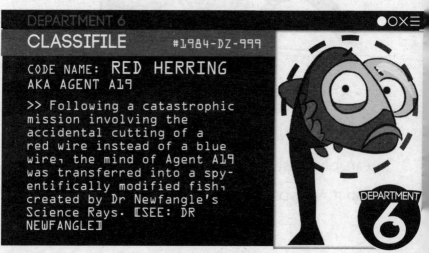

"What's going on?" asked Red Herring, circling her fishbowl defensively. "Because whatever it is, I didn't do it."

"There's something fishy about you, fish!" said Danger Monkey, dropping Holey Moley and picking up Red Herring's fishbowl. "What are you so nervous about? Are you a mole, Herring?"

"Why would I turn traitor?" Red Herring replied. "What do you think, that I'm secretly resentful of Department 6 because they brought me back as a fish? I mean, a *fish*! Do you know what the job prospects are for a secret agent who can't breathe out of water? It's enough to make me betray everything and everyone I hold dear! Also, I'm totally innocent."

"Mole!" Danger Monkey howled. "Tell us everythin' or I'll mash yer potatoes! I'll dice yer carrots! I'll sauté yer onions!"

"Steady on, Danger Monkey — things are not always as they seem," said Spynosaur. "Like a door marked 'Sweet Shop This Way' that actually leads to a pit of man-eating cyber-gators."

"Da-ad, I only fell for that once," mumbled an embarrassed Amber, scuffing the floor with her foot.

"The point is, Red Herring's a red herring — the *real* mole just stole a spycycle and fled down that tunnel," Spynosaur replied. Sure enough, one of the spycycles was missing ... and Holey Moley was nowhere to be seen.

"Well, this is awkward..." muttered Danger Monkey, replacing Red Herring's bowl on her platform. He puffed on the bowl and polished it with his elbow. "No 'ard feelin's, yeah?"

"Like Grandma Gambit's soup, the plot thickens fast," Spynosaur said, pacing around the room. "Henchmen galore ... betrayed by Goldkey© ... Shady Lady sprung from captivity... My super-spy senses are telling me this is the work of a mysterious *new* criminal mastermind. And what a *diabolical* villain he must be."

"Blast it to smithereens, Spynosaur! This is more confusing than the settings on my electric moustache comb!" M11 cried. "Now, are you going to crack this case or — as is my personal preference — retire to the countryside and leave spying to those of us who are up to the job?"

"We'll crack it!" cried Amber, adding hopefully, "Right, Dad?"

"Time we did some *digging* around," Spynosaur replied, peering into the pitch-black tunnel. He took the other spycycle off the wall and climbed on to it. "Let's see how deep this mole-hole goes."

# 9.
# GOLD RUSHED

 **DEEP BENEATH THE STREETS OF LONDON**

Amber clung on to Spynosaur's back as he rode the spycycle through the tunnel.

**DEPARTMENT 6**                                        ●○○✕☰

**CLASSIFILE**       #1984-DZ-999

CODE NAME: **SPYCYCLE**

>> High-powered, jet-
propelled, impractically
loud, top-secret motorcycle.
Specially adaptable for
riders of all shapes and
sizes - even those lacking
opposable thumbs.

DEPARTMENT
**6**

They'd been speeding through the darkness for over an hour in pursuit of Holey Moley, the spycycle's bright headlights illuminating thousands of tiny flecks of gold, scraped off the Gold Digger's hull.

"Whoever this new villain is, they *really* like gold!" Amber shouted over her dad's shoulder.

"Gold's always been a popular theme for criminals," Spynosaur explained. "There's Golden Oldie, Solid Gold, Gilded Mildred ... but it can't be any of them – I made sure they all ... retired."

MISSION #7 // GOLDEN OLDIE

MISSION #23 // SOLID GOLD

MISSION #43 // GILDED MILDRED

"No, this has to be some new nemesis," Spynosaur continued, his scaly skin goose-bumped with excitement. "Unknowable, unpredictable, diabolical. An enemy worthy of my spy-skills! Talk about a *golden* opportunity..."

Amber couldn't believe how happy it made her to hear her dad making bad puns. It seemed like even just the promise of a genuine criminal mastermind had brought him back to his old self. Amber crossed her fingers and hoped this new villain would turn out to be the most diablolical they'd ever met.

"But what do they want with Shady Lady?" Amber began. "Why free her and not— Holey Moley!"

"Well spotted, Amber – I see him!" said Spynosaur, spying the other spycycle as it raced ahead of them in the tunnel. He accelerated fast, using his uncanny skills to traverse the unpredictable terrain.

"We've almost got him! Faster!" Amber cried.

"My super-spy senses tell me something's not right – and they're never wrong," said Spynosaur, craning his scaly head to listen. "Sounds like ... something diabolical. Sounds like..."

"Like what?" said Amber, as a low rumbling sound filled the walls of the tunnel, growing louder by the second. Then she spotted something ahead – a strange, golden glow. Amber squinted into the darkness.

A wall of churning, liquid gold was rushing towards them at high speed.

"Like a golden tidal wave!" Spynosaur cried. He spun the spycycle round on its back wheel, as the deafening torrent of liquid raced towards them.

"Get us out of here!" cried Amber, daring to glance back. "Hit the rocket boo—"

SOMEWHERE UNDERGROUND

"Wuuh...?"

Amber opened her eyes and looked around. She found herself in a wide, windowless, entirely golden hall, with curved golden walls and a golden floor. She was seated at a golden table, laid with a golden dinner service and golden food. Round the table were several chairs, distinctly golden in appearance. And seated at the other end of the table...

"Dad!" Amber cried.

79

"No sudden moves, Amber, there's a good girl," said Spynosaur. He pointed to the bearded Goldkey© chief and numerous henchmen covering every exit of the golden room. They carried hi-tech machine guns, the golden dots of their laser-scopes dancing across Spynosaur and Amber's spy-suits.

"Where are we?" Amber asked, surprised not to find a scratch on her. "I thought we'd drowned but now I'm not even damp! What's going on?"

"There are two possibilities," her dad replied.

"One: in our pursuit of the mole we edged too close to the villain's secret underground lair, thus activating its defence mechanism – a golden tidal wave which, in truth, is not liquid at all but rather a synthetic substance comprising billions of robotic nano-droplets capable of moving in any direction its master commands, as well as rendering its victims unconscious. The golden wave conveyed us here to the hidden underground lair of my soon-to-be arch-enemy, the mysterious criminal mastermind. Or two: it's all a dream."

"Holey Moley!" Amber cried.

"Yes, my brain *is* surprisingly impressive," Spynosaur concluded.

"No ... *look*!" Amber whispered. Sure enough, Holey Moley's tiny head poked cautiously over the top of the table, as he dangled precariously from his claws.

"Shhh! They haven't spotted me!" Holey Moley whispered. He gestured towards the Goldkey© henchmen, still oblivious to his presence. "I'm here to help!"

"*Help?*" Amber repeated in hushed tones. "This is all your fault, you Department-deceiving, double-crossing mole!"

"I'm not a mole!" insisted Holey Moley. "I mean, obviously I'm a— The point is, this has nothing to do with me! I'm as loyal as the next agent, I swear I am."

"Swearing you're *not* a mole is exactly what a mole would say," snarled Amber. "It says so in the How to Spot a Mole Handbook!"

## IDENTIFYING A MOLE, DOUBLE AGENT, TRAITOR OR TURNCOAT

1. Does the suspected mole claim they are not a mole?
NO – probably a mole
YES – almost certainly a mole

"Amber has a point," whispered Spynosaur. "Secret agents with nothing to hide don't disappear down dark tunnels..."

"It's the mole in me! I mean, the *actual* mole — these days whenever things get too much I feel compelled to disappear underground into some tunnel or other," replied Holey Moley. "With all the accusations flying around, I panicked! I saw the tunnel and I couldn't help myself..."

"Classic mole talk," hissed Amber. "Once we get out of this I'm going to ninja-kick you right in the—"

# KRUNG-VRRRRRRR!

"It's the boss!" barked the chief. The henchmen stood to attention.

"*Finally*," Spynosaur said. "My new nemesis."

At the far end of the hall a wide, curved door slid open. Holey Moley scurried fearfully under the table and Amber saw her dad sit up in anticipation.

"Doo-dooo, doo-dooo..."

Amber had to admit, the man who trotted into the hall humming an inoffensive tune wasn't what she expected from an arch-enemy. He was short and round – barely taller than Amber – and wore a plain brown suit and thick glasses. What little there was left of his dyed-black hair puffed out over his ears like tiny clouds.

"I'm so sorry, I hope my Gold Rush wave wasn't too rough on you – my scientists are still working out the kinks..." he said, waving a gold control pad held in his palm.

"*Diabolical,*" said Spynosaur, flashing his sharp teeth.

"They think all the gold might be affecting its nano-circuitry," the man continued. "It's funny, you pick a theme on a whim then you're stuck with it! If I'd have known how difficult gold was to work with, I might have picked something else. Still, too late now..."

Spynosaur got to his feet. The golden dots of the henchmen's laser-scopes trained on his chest as he loomed over the small man.

"The name's Spynosaur," he said, glowering at his new enemy through keen, lizard eyes. "And you are?"

"Such a pleasure!" replied the man, straightening

his tie. "My name is Graham. Graham Goldentoe."

"Golden ... toe?" repeated Amber. She could think of a hundred more villainous names off the top of her head.

"And before you ask, yes, it's my real name!" chuckled Goldentoe. "But by sheer coincidence it is particularly fitting, as a result of a minor accident in a jewellery shop in Hatton Garden."

He took off the shoe and sock on his right foot and lifted his foot on to the table to reveal a gleaming gold toe.

"Eww!" said Amber.

"What do you want, Goldentoe?" growled Spynosaur, slamming a clawed fist against the table. "To wreak chaos and destruction on the world? To hold governments to ransom? To conquer the globe through nefarious means? Or simply to do battle with your nemesis ... namely, me."

"Ah, what I want cannot be put into words," insisted Goldentoe.

"Even if the words are 'criminal' and 'mastermind'?" Spynosaur replied.

"And don't forget 'diabolical'!" Amber added enthusiastically.

"Follow me and I'll shed some light on it," Goldentoe replied, brandishing his control pad. "Or should I say, *darkness*."

# 11.
# GOLDENTOE'S (DIABOLICAL?) PLAN

"Dooo-doo, doo-doo..." Goldentoe hummed as he made his way slowly across the vast, golden hall. As Spynosaur followed, Amber glanced under the table to check for Holey Moley but he was nowhere to be seen. She swore a bucketload of revenge on him before hurrying to join her dad.

"Money!" cried Goldentoe, pressing a button on his control pad. "Making it is the only thing I've ever been good at, which is helpful when you've got a lot of science stuff to pay for..."

With a **KER-RUNG**, the far wall of the hall

dropped through the floor to reveal a vast golden hangar filled with Goldentoe's eye-blindingly shiny arsenal of inventions, from his Gold Digger drill-tanks to golden jet-copters to a huge vertical cylinder containing the Gold Rush liquid that had engulfed Spynosaur and Amber in the tunnel. Dozens of scientists and engineers in golden jumpsuits busied themselves about the hangar, making sure everything was in working order.

"I hate to burst your bubble, Goldentoe," began Spynosaur, striking a dramatic pose, "but I won't let you carry out your diabolical plan to wreak global havoc and/or take over the world."

"Take over? Havoc? Plan? The?" said Goldentoe. He pressed another button on his control pad. "I'm afraid you're not quite getting it. All will become clear when I reveal the guest of honour!"

Behind them in the hall, yet another wall fell away to reveal yet another insistently golden room. It was decked out with an array of ornate gold furniture and in its centre, still shrouded in shadow despite her relentlessly gleaming surroundings, was Shady Lady.

"What's the meaning of this madness? What loon liberated me just to lock me up again?" hissed Shady Lady, sweeping into the hall like a spectre.

"My sincere apologies for keeping you waiting," explained Goldentoe. "I just wanted to make sure everything was ready for you." He bowed his head. "And may I say how nice it is to see you again..."

"Of course! The final piece of the puzzle falls into place," declared Spynosaur. "This was your plan all along — a villainous team-up! Goldentoe and Shady Lady ... the diabolical duo dedicated to taking over the world!"

"What waffle," Shady Lady tutted. "I've never met this man in my life."

"You – you don't remember me? Ah, well... No, I don't blame you," said Goldentoe, clearly deflated. "As it happens, we spent six years together, in the same class at school."

"You two were at *school* together?" Amber blurted.

"Goldentoe..." muttered Shady Lady, wracking her brain. "I remember! Graham Goldentoe... The class called you 'Graham Boring Pants'..."

Goldentoe forced a chuckle and fixed his gaze upon Shady Lady. "Ever since the day we first met, I knew you were different from the other children. They used to throw pencils at me, put chewing gum on my chair, flush my head down the toilet ... you were the only one who ignored me completely."

"Don't take it personally," Shady Lady said with

a shrug. "I had pernicious plots to perfect."

"It was back then I realized what I was meant to do with my life," Goldentoe added.

"Become a diabolical villain!" declared Spynosaur.

"Me, a villain? Perish the thought!" Goldentoe guffawed. He turned to Shady Lady, and fell upon one knee in front of her. "I did all this for you, Shady Lady ... I did it all for *love*!"

# 12.
# UN-SPY-ENTIFIC USES FOR A RAY EMITTER

"Did you say ... love?" Spynosaur uttered as the truth began to dawn on him – Goldentoe was driven by the least villainous emotion *ever*. He wasn't an evil criminal mastermind at all – he was just in love with one.

"I spent my life becoming rich and powerful so I could be the man you deserved," explained Goldentoe, peering longingly into Shady Lady's eyes. "Someone who could give you everything you wanted ... protect you from your enemies ... free you whenever you got caught! I did all this for you – all for love!" said Goldentoe.

"All for love..." Spynosaur repeated.

Amber looked up at her dad and her heart sank – he had that lost look in his eyes once more.

"And I got you a present!" Goldentoe continued. "Something even money can't buy – the key to defeating your enemies! Or whatever it is villains like to do..." He pressed his control pad again and one of the Gold Diggers rolled out of the hangar into the hall. Its doors whirred open and the ramp slid out from inside, depositing Dr Newfangle's Ray Emitter on to the floor.

"He stole Ronald Ray-Gun!" Amber cried, prodding her dad in the arm. "See, Dad, he's a complete stinker! One hundred per cent villain!"

But Spynosaur just stared into the middle distance and said:

"When's a villain not a villain?
When love shines in his eyes.
But if villains are not villains,
What use have we for spies?"

"So what do you say, Shady Lady?" continued Goldentoe on bended knee. "Will you give me ... will you give *us* a chance?"

Shady Lady stared at Goldentoe for a long moment, and then said, "No."

"Oh, that's wonderful! You don't know how happy it makes me to— Wait, 'No'?" spluttered Goldentoe. "But all this ... I did it all for you! The henchmen! The tanks! The helicopters! I-I had golden toilet paper made!"

"Look, I'm shockingly shallow and you're wildly wealthy – it ought to be enough," Shady Lady explained. "But you're just not my type."

"It's not me, Graham, it's you," explained Shady Lady. "You do wrong things for the right reasons. Deep down, you're decent. Why, you're as good as gold." She opened her hand to reveal Spynosaur's tooth. "But I am drawn to *danger* – and you'll never be dangerous like a dinosaur."

"Wait ... dinosaur?" Amber muttered, following Shady Lady's admiring glance at Spynosaur. She suddenly remembered Newfangle's words back in the Vault...

*"An enemy could form, fashion, transmute or transmogrify whatever they pleased – even a dinosaur!"*

In an instant, an idea occurred to her, which immediately became a plan. Then this happened:

# "INSPIRED SWIFT ALBATROSS PAPERBACK KICK!"

In a blur of movement, Amber ninja-kicked Spynosaur's tooth from Shady Lady's hand. It flew across the room and landed by Goldentoe's feet.

"Amber, what...?" Spynosaur said, snapping out of his gloom as Goldentoe picked up the tooth and peered at it.

"Hey, Goldentoe, you want the tooth? You can't handle the tooth!" Amber cried. "You'll never be dangerous without dino-DNA and a blast of Science Rays!"

"Dangerous...?" murmured Goldentoe. He looked over at the Ray Emitter, then at the tooth resting in his palm. His eyes grew wide. "I can be dangerous!" he cried, leaping to his feet and racing to the Ray Emitter. He quickly turned the dial to "Transmute". The machine hummed into life, as Goldentoe aimed the barrel directly at himself.

"Goldentoe, no!" shouted Spynosaur.

But it was too late.

ZEEEEEEEEE

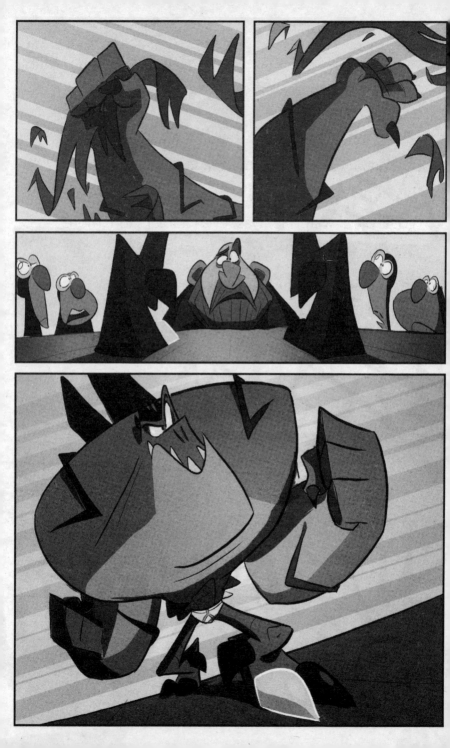

"*Perfect,*" noted an impressed Amber, as a grotesque half-human, half-dinosaur stepped forwards on clawed feet. The creature inspected his repulsive reflection in the mirror-polished gold of a wall. He was even larger and more imposing than her dad, his appearance savagely saurian with just a hint of Goldentoe's humanity.

"Dangerous..." growled the man-monster, admiring his monstrousness.

"Dad, look! Goldentoe used your tooth – and the mysterious power of science rays – to combine his DNA with yours!" Amber cried dramatically. "Totally transmuted!"

"B-Boss?" said the Goldkey© chief, nervously taking a step towards the beast. "Goldentoe, is that you?"

"Graham Goldentoe is no more," replied the monster. "Call me ... **GOLDENCLAW!**"

# 13.
# SPYNOSAUR VS GOLDENCLAW (ROUND 1)

FROM THE DEPTHS OF DESPERATION COMES A **VILLAIN** FOR TODAY, TRANSFORMED INTO **A MONSTER** WITH A **SUPER SCIENCE RAY.**

HE'S PARTLY PREHISTORIC AND HE'S SLIGHTLY MODERN MAN, BUT WE'LL HAVE TO WAIT A WHILE BEFORE WE LEARN HIS **EVIL PLAN**

# GOLDENCLAW!

"Instant nemesis – just add Ronald Ray-Gun," said Amber, proudly inspecting the monster calling itself Goldenclaw. Surely her dad couldn't have asked for a more impressive-looking villain. Amber just hoped he had what it took to be a real arch-enemy ... and there was only one way to find out.

"Hey, Graham! You think a *makeover's* enough to make you dangerous?" Amber cried. "My dad could still beat you up with his tail tied behind his back and a case of the sniffles!"

"Amber! What are you doing?" Spynosaur blurted, looking less delighted than Amber hoped at the sight of his new nemesis.

"Dangerous? I'll show you dangerous," said Goldenclaw. His own henchmen backed away as he wheeled round and headed for Spynosaur. "I'll show you dangerous!"

"Go get him, Dad!" Amber cried excitedly as Spynosaur and Goldenclaw raced towards each other. "And you're welcome!"

Amber's jaw fell open as she watched Goldenclaw rain down blows upon her dad. Spynosaur didn't get in a single strike — it was all he could do to defend himself from an onslaught of fists, feet, teeth and claws. Within seconds, Goldenclaw's relentless attack sent Spynosaur crumpling to the floor.

"There's a new dinosaur in town, Spynosaur — it looks like you need to *evolve*," growled Goldenclaw. He swung his tail, swatting Spynosaur across the room.

"Dad!" Amber cried. Without thinking, she raced towards Goldenclaw.

"**TORNADO SOCK PUPPET SURPRISING GOBLIN ATTA**— ungh!" cried Amber, leaping into the air, but Goldenclaw countered her ninja-move so swiftly that Amber found herself skittering along the ground — helpless to avoid his swift-swinging tail.

Goldenclaw turned back to Shady Lady. "Look at what I have done for you, Lady... Look at what I've become for you. *Now* will you be mine?" He held out his clawed hands in front of her face.

"Flattening my foes is fantastically flattering," said Shady Lady, already seeing the potential in an unstoppable man-monster who worshipped the ground she walked on. "But I'm horribly high-maintenance. I've made a vow of villainy. Love me, love my lawlessness..."

"I can do that!" cried Goldenclaw. He tapped the side of his head with a clawed finger. "I've changed – everything makes sense now. I know how to prove myself to you!"

"Boss!"

The chief's cry echoed around the lair. Goldenclaw turned and saw Amber desperately dragging her unconscious father up the ramp of the nearby Gold Digger.

"Finish them," Goldenclaw grunted.

The Goldkey© henchmen aimed their weapons. There was no way Amber could close the Gold Digger's ramp in time.

"Can I help?" came a sudden squeak. Up on the table at the other end of the hall stood Holey Moley. In his tiny claws he held Goldenclaw's control pad, retrieved from Goldentoe's shredded jacket.

"Holey Moley...?" muttered Amber, and heard the mole cry, "Go! Go!" With that, he pressed a button on the control pad; at the other end of the hangar, the towering 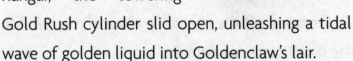 Gold Rush cylinder slid open, unleashing a tidal wave of golden liquid into Goldenclaw's lair.

"No!" growled Goldenclaw, as the wave

engulfed the hangar and raced towards the hall.

Amber slammed her fist against the Gold Digger's door controls.

"Wait...!" wheezed a voice.

Spynosaur stirred! As the Gold Digger's cargo doors began to close, he weakly drew his grapple-gun and fired. The grappling hook streaked forth, skewering Shady Lady's ink-black dress. As the Gold-Rush wave loomed over her, Spynosaur retracted the hook. In an instant, Shady Lady was dragged across the room and inside the Gold Digger, a split-second before the cargo doors slammed shut.

"NO!" roared Goldenclaw again – but it was too late. The torrent engulfed the hall. As it swept Holey Moley, the Goldkey© henchmen and even Goldenclaw off their feet, Spynosaur reached for the Gold Digger's controls...

# 14

# GRANDMA GAMBIT

## TROUSERFALL LODGE, THE HIGHLANDS OF IRELAND

"Whuhh...?"

Spynosaur opened his eyes. He tried to move, but found he had aches and pains in places he didn't even know you could get aches and pains.

"How are you feeling?" said a voice.

Spynosaur turned his head to see an old woman with hair as white as milk and teeth as yellow as cheese.

"Grandma?" Spynosaur said, managing to sit up. "Where – *oww* – where am I?"

"Blowed if I know," Grandma Gambit replied. "I can barely remember me own name these days."

"Trouserfall Lodge!" cried Spynosaur, looking around. He squinted as the morning sun shone through a dozen cracked windows. The house he grew up in was just as he remembered it – as dusty and dilapidated as Grandma Gambit herself. "But how did I—?"

"Sure, it's no use asking me, poppet – the old memory's not what it was," replied Grandma Gambit with a shrug. "At least it means life's full of surprises! Tell me, have you always been a dinosaur?"

"It's a long story, Grandma," confessed Spynosaur.

"Don't waste your time, then, I'll have forgotten it by dinner," Grandma Gambit said. "Would you care for some soup?"

"Dad!" came a sudden cry. Amber rushed in from the kitchen and hugged her dad so hard he squealed in pain.

"What – oww – what happened?" Spynosaur asked. "How did we get to Trouserfall?"

"While everyone was getting gold-rushed, you dug us an escape route," Amber replied. "And then you put some coordinates into the Gold Digger so it'd bring us here. And then you made sure I was OK and gave me a hug. And then you passed out."

"Sounds like the sort of wildly impressive thing I'd do," said Spynosaur. He glanced out of the window to see one of Goldenclaw's Gold Diggers parked on the drive. "How long was I out?"

Amber counted on her fingers. "Three days."

"*Three days!*" cried Spynosaur. "M11 must be going *spare.*"

"I tried to call in but I can't get a signal *anywhere,*" Amber added, tapping her Super Secret Spy Watch™ in frustration. "I've even tried climbing on to the roof..."

"Amber Gambit, a loose roof tile underfoot is an accident waiting to happen," Spynosaur admonished. "You wouldn't have had any luck anyway – Trouserfall Lodge is unreachable and undetectable. There's so much stealth technology wired into this house, even M11 doesn't know about it. When a spy doesn't want to be found, they come here. Isn't that right, Grandma?"

"Blowed if I remember," replied Grandma Gambit with a shrug.

"Still, three days is as long as I've ever gone without doing something unfeasibly impressive," exclaimed Spynosaur. He leaped to his feet – and immediately fell face-first on to the floor. "There is a very slight possibility I'm not back to full strength," he noted.

"I'm so sorry, Dad!" Amber rushed to him, tears welling up in her eyes. "I thought if Goldentoe could be a proper nemesis, you'd go back to your old self ... but I didn't think he'd hurt you. I didn't think *anything* could hurt you." Amber helped her dad sit up. "I thought you didn't want to spy any more. I thought you were giving up."

"*That's* why you urged Goldentoe to turn himself into that monster?" Spynosaur asked. He shook his head. "Perhaps I have been feeling a bit sorry for myself lately..."

"A bit of a lot..." Amber replied with a sniff. "You've been a total *downer-saur*."

"Pun taken," said her dad with a grin. "Well, the navel-gazing stops now ... not that dinosaurs have navels."

"So, you're not going to give up spying?" Amber asked.

Spynosaur wiped the tears from her eyes with a clawed finger. "Amber, even if we run out of villains altogether – even if the world no longer needs Spynosaur – I'll never give this up. Being a spy means I get to spend time with *you*." Amber's dad gave her a hug, and added, "But no more poetry, I promise."

"Shame. I like a good limerick," Grandma Gambit interrupted. "There once was a man from Caerphilly, who liked to do things that were silly. He travelled to France, pulled down his pants and... Sure, I don't remember the rest."

"Holey Moley!" Amber said. "He saved us back in Goldenclaw's lair, which means..."

"Which means the mole is not a mole," Spynosaur mused, raising a scaly eyebrow. "The real mole is still at large, while Holy Moley is most likely Goldenclaw's prisoner. Don't worry, it's all on my to-do list." He got to his feet with a pained grunt. "But first things first – what on earth did you do with Shady Lady?"

# 15.
# MOVING HOUSE

Spynosaur, Amber and Grandma Gambit made their way through the house and into the garage. On a chair in the middle of the floor sat Shady Lady, bound by ropes and snoring loudly.

"Who's this? You never told me we had guests," said Grandma Gambit. She retrieved an upturned soup bowl from the floor and then prodded Shady Lady in the arm.

"Spynosaur...?" murmured Shady Lady, catching sight of the spy as she came to. "I'm delighted you deigned not to die ... between that baffled biddy and your despairing daughter, there's been a shocking shortage of cogent conversation."

"Shut up, you stinker, or I'll tighten those ropes again!" Amber snapped.

"Ropes? *Really...*" Shady Lady exclaimed. She stood up, and her ropes fell loosely to the floor. "Didn't you know? I'm a dab hand at disentanglement. I'd have departed days ago if that dotty old dear hadn't *drugged* my dinner..."

"Who, me? Sure, I'd have remembered doing something like that," said Grandma Gambit, handing the soup bowl to Amber with a wink. "Right! I'm off to prune the hedges. Which way to the garden?"

As Amber pointed Grandma Gambit in the direction of the garden, Shady Lady sidled up to Spynosaur.

"You *must* have a more immediate mission than me," she said, resting a hand upon his chest. "If I positively promise not to misbehave or make even a modicum of mischief, maybe you'd let me go...?"

"Sorry, Shady Lady, but I can't risk Goldenclaw getting his hands on you," he explained. "You think you can use him to help you take over the criminal underworld ... but he won't stop there."

"So you say," replied Shady Lady. "*I* think you fear a foe of such formidable ferocity."

"Of course he's formidable – he's part me," Spynosaur said. "But that means he also has my more ... *prehistoric* impulses – what Amber charmingly refers to as my *dino-side*."

"We've fought before, Spynosaur – I've seen your savage state. You're *fabulously* fearsome," cooed Shady Lady. "Why, if I remember rightly, last time we tussled you came quite close to swallowing your so-called sidekick."

"He was being mind-controlled by Ergo Ego that time!" shouted Amber. "Also, shut up!"

"The point is, Goldenclaw has none of my training, none of my willpower, none of my singularly impressive self-control," Spynosaur concluded. "He's monstrous ... dangerous ... 'diabolical' with a capital 'D', and possibly a capital 'IABOLICAL.'"

"Sounds sublime," replied Shady Lady.

"Do you really think Goldenclaw's gone bad, Dad?" Amber asked, with renewed guilt at her part in his transformation. "I just thought he wanted Shady Lady to go out with him."

"Precisely, Amber – Goldenclaw is determined to prove himself a villain, and that is why he is so dangerous," Spynosaur explained. "Our mission is to keep Shady Lady as far away from Goldenclaw as possible. Whatever he's planning, he'll want Shady by his side, bearing witness to his mad— Wait."

Spynosaur tilted his head to listen.

"I hear it, too!" Amber cried. "Something's *coming*. Something—"

**KRUNNG-CH!**

The sound rattled the walls of the garage and sent dust falling from the ceiling. Then:

**KRONNG-CH!**
**KRUNNG-CH!**

"Ah, the certain sound of jet-copter-mounted reinforced grappling cables," said Shady Lady. "I suspect I'm saved."

"We're — we're moving!" Amber screamed, as everything began to shake.

"Yes, moving *house*," added Spynosaur. "Hang on to something!" A moment later the entire building was torn from its foundations. Everyone fell to the floor as the house swung back and forth, before rising into the air.

From the garden, Grandma Gambit watched

as four gleaming, golden jet-copters lifted Trouserfall Lodge from the ground via clawed cables and carried it off into the air.

"Sure, there's something you don't see every day," she said, as Trouserfall disappeared into the clouds. "I wonder whose house that is?"

# 16.
# HOUSE GUESTS

"I'd say Goldenclaw is well and truly *hooked* on you, Shady Lady," noted Spynosaur, as he, Amber and Shady Lady raced through the garage into Trouserfall's dusty sitting room. Spynosaur poked his head out of the window and looked up. High above him, four golden jet-copters conveyed Trouserfall Lodge through the sky on long grappling cables.

"How did he find us?" cried Amber. "I thought you said Trouserfall was in stealth mode!"

"Don't forget, Goldenclaw has a hefty dollop of my DNA," Spynosaur said. "That makes him almost as breathtakingly impressive as—"

# KASH! CHASH! KA-TASSH!

Henchmen crashed through the windows, swinging down on metallic golden cables. But these were not the foes Spynosaur had faced before – they had been altogether changed by the Ray Emitter's transmutation beam. Amber counted six half-human *henchimals* resembling a bear, a tiger, a hippo, a cheetah, a hyena – even a feathered falcon.

"Henchmen upgrades! I knew I had animal magnetism but this is ridiculous," said Spynosaur, cracking his knuckles. "Let's see what they've got, shall we?"

WHEN HIS DNA'S BEEN STOLEN AND OUR HERO'S BEEN DEFEATED

YOU'D THINK HE MIGHT FEEL BAD ABOUT THE WAY HE'S BEEN MISTREATED

"Is that the *beast* you've got?" said Spynosaur as the last of the henchimals fell unconscious to the floor. Spynosaur and Amber blew on their bruised knuckles.

"What a disappointingly deft defeat," Shady Lady tutted. "I hope my beastly beau has something spectacular up his slee—"

In a sudden flash of bright light, a huge hole appeared in the ceiling above them. Spynosaur, Amber and Shady Lady looked up. The hole extended all the way into the sky and there, hanging out of the open door of one of the jet-copters and brandishing the Ray Emitter like a weapon, was Goldenclaw.

"He's got Ronald Ray-Gun up there!" Amber cried.

"Disintegration Ray — diabolical," noted Spynosaur. "He's certainly got to grips with the Ray Emitter..."

"Lady! I find myself drawn to you!" growled Goldenclaw over the noisy WHUP-WHUP of the jet-copters. He turned the Ray Emitter's Science Dial. "Are you not drawn to me, too?"

"'Drawn to'...? The Gravity Ray!" cried Spynosaur. "Amber! Switcheroo!"

"Switcheroo?" Amber blurted. "But—"

"Now!" Spynosaur ordered.

In that moment, Goldenclaw activated the Ray Emitter's gravity-defying energy beam — it struck Shady Lady, pulling her off her feet and into the air. She floated helplessly through the hole in the ceiling and out into the air.

"Goldenclaw! How did you find me?" snapped Shady Lady, as Goldenclaw reached out and grabbed her by the arm.

"I followed my heart!" Goldenclaw replied, pulling her inside the jet-copter. "I mean, the tracking device in the Gold Digger helped, but mostly I followed ... my..." Goldenclaw fell silent as he peered at Shady Lady. "There's ... there's something *different* about you," he added suspiciously. Shady Lady flashed a surprisingly sharp-toothed grin, a glint in her oddly yellow and lizard-like eyes.

"I had my hair done," she replied.

"Boss! Are we good to go?" cried the chief (who'd been transformed into a hulking part-man, part-orangutan and looked hairier than ever) from the pilot seat.

"Not before we lighten the load," said Goldenclaw with a sharp-toothed grin. "Chief! Release the cables! Drop them!"

Shady Lady clenched her fists as she heard the jet-copter's grappling cables release their golden grip on the house.

A moment later, Trouserfall Lodge plummeted to the ground.

# 17.
# SPYTANIUM

 ABOARD GOLDENCLAW'S
GOLDEN JET-COPTER

"You'll pay for that, Goldenclaw," insisted Shady
Lady, as Goldenclaw's jet-copter split from the
convoy and headed in the opposite direction.
"Defeating villains like you is what Spynosaur does
for a living ... and occasionally for a hobby. He also
said you were bound to have come up with some
insane plan to impress me. So, what is it?"

"Oh, you'll see," Goldenclaw replied. He patted
the Ray Emitter and let out a snorting laugh. "Make

yourself comfortable, Lady – we have quite a trip ahead. Tell me, have you ever been to Tibet?"

Hours later, the setting sun had turned the sky red as the jet-copter came to land outside a vast, hidden temple deep within the Tibetan jungle. The temple, overgrown with foliage, stretched high into the air, almost clearing the dense canopy of green forest that stretched for miles in every direction.

"Doo-dooo, doo-doo," Goldenclaw hummed. He slid open the jet-copter's door and aimed the Ray Emitter at the temple door.

"This looks familiar..." muttered Shady Lady.

"Impossible – I have it on good authority that no one's been to this temple for thousands of years – no one except Spynosaur," replied Goldenclaw, switching the Science Dial to Reduction Ray.

A single blast reduced the temple's stone door to the size of a lunch box, leaving in its place a gaping doorway.

"That's one way to *make an entrance*," noted Shady Lady. Goldenclaw climbed down from the jet-copter and made his way towards the temple, gesturing for Shady Lady to follow. As she hurried after him, Shady Lady added, "I assume this 'good authority' is the mole in Department 6. Tell me, who exactly is—?"

Shady Lady's jaw fell open. There, poking out of the back of Goldenclaw's striped underpants (and doing his best to stay hidden) was Holey Moley.

"*Holey Moley!*" Shady Lady silently mouthed. The mole panicked, sure that Shady Lady was about to reveal his position ... but instead, she winked and mouthed, "*Shhh.*"

"All will become clear, Lady," said Goldenclaw as they entered the temple. It was dark, dank and empty but for a large, glowing red rock atop a plinth in the centre of the room. Goldenclaw plucked the rock from the plinth and held it up.

"*Spytanium*," he said. "This remarkable element is the secret to the Ray Emitter's power. It takes only the tiniest fragment of spytanium to charge it for a *lifetime*. It's so powerful that even the spy-entists of Department 6 cannot be trusted with it. That's why M11 ordered Spynosaur to hide the Spytanium here ... in case someone was tempted to abuse its power."

"And yet *you* knew exactly where to look for it," said Shady Lady. "Anyway, you should have done your research – that much spytanium will overload Ronald Ray-Gun in seconds."

"You need to think big, Lady – didn't I tell you I have a plan? Didn't I say I was going to prove myself to you?" Goldenclaw replied, his horrifying visage illuminated by the spytanium rock. He leaned closer, until Shady Lady felt his breath upon her face. "And may I say, you've never looked so beautiful... Your eyes are as yellow as the sun, your skin is as green as the jungle, your tail as long as— Wait, *tail*?"

"Surprise," said Shady Lady. Goldenclaw staggered back in horror as she tore off her disguise, to reveal the world's first and only super secret agent dinosaur.

"SPYNOSAUR! But how...?" boomed Goldenclaw.

"The *Switcheroo* — the oldest trick in the book with the word 'switcheroo' in its name," replied Spynosaur. "I thought it prudent to pick up a Shady Lady disguise back at HQ. The second before you activated the Gravity Ray back in Trouserfall Lodge, I used my quick-change training to don the disguise and switch places with Shady Lady."

"You — you mean I dropped her?" cried a horrified Goldenclaw. "I *dropped* Shady Lady?"

"Like a stone," replied Spynosaur. "Fortunately I also found time to slip my sidekick a handy gadget..."

"So you see, Amber and Shady Lady are as safe as *houses*," explained Spynosaur as Goldenclaw loomed over him. "Or, in the case of my poor family home, considerably safer."

"Where is Shady Lady? WHERE? What have you done with her?" Goldenclaw roared. "Tell me, or I'll crush every bone in your— Aah!"

Suddenly Goldenclaw began hopping wildly from foot to gold-clawed foot. He thrust his hands down the back of his underpants, rummaging around like a man-monster possessed.

"There's something ... down there!" Goldenclaw howled, dropping the spytanium and shoving his other hand down his pants. "Get it out! Get it out!"

"Excellent work, Agent Moley," said Spynosaur, retrieving the spytanium from the ground.

"I'm helping! Am I helping?" the mole squeaked from inside Goldenclaw's underwear.

"You certainly are," Spynosaur grinned. Then he clenched his other fist and drew it back. "Round two, Goldenclaw."

THWUMP!

# 18.
# SPYNOSAUR VS GOLDENCLAW
# (ROUND 2)

Goldenclaw didn't even see the blow coming – Spynosaur's bone-crunching punch sent him flying across the temple and out of the entrance. Goldenclaw bounced along the ground until he collided with a tree, striking it with such force that it fell to the jungle floor.

"How's that for a *punch*line?" said Spynosaur, unclenching his fist and shaking his hand.

"Told you – *urf* – I'm not the mole..." squeaked Holey Moley, dragging himself out from underneath Goldenclaw's limp body.

"I never doubted you for more than an hour or so, Moley," said Spynosaur. "Have you been concealing yourself in Goldenclaw's undergarments for all this time?"

"I panicked! After the Gold Rush subsided, I just looked for somewhere dark to hide," squeaked Holey Moley. "It wasn't so bad ... although three days is a long time to be nestled between two scaly—"

"Spynosaur!" came a cry. Spynosaur spun round to see Goldenclaw drag himself to his feet. He spat out a couple of teeth and clenched his fists. "You'll have to do better than a sucker punch. I defeated you once, I can do it again!"

"Which is exactly why I evened the odds," Spynosaur replied, flashing his Super Secret Spy Watch™. As the leaves of the trees began to shake, Goldenclaw looked up to see Spynosaur's Dino-soarer descending from the sky. Behind it, half a dozen Department 6 jets hovered in the air, their weapons trained upon Goldenclaw.

"Nobody move a claw!" cried Danger Monkey over the Dino-soarer's loudspeaker. "Anyone tries anything and I'll fry yer like an egg! I'll cook yer in your own juices! I'll marinade yer with assorted herbs an' spices!"

Goldenclaw roared in desperate defiance. He glanced back to see the chief leap out of the jet-copter and flee into the forest with a simian howl. Goldenclaw paused for a moment ... then he raised his clawed hands in surrender.

"Dad, are you all right?" added Amber, waving from the Dino-soarer's cockpit.

"Never better," he replied, his grin illuminated by the spytanium. "I'd say that's mission accomplished, wouldn't you?"

# 19

# SHADY DEALINGS

## HIGH ABOVE THE NORTH ATLANTIC OCEAN

Soon Spynosaur, Amber, Danger Monkey and Holey Moley were aboard the Dino-soarer, heading back to Department 6 headquarters — with the Ray Emitter and the spytanium safely on board.

In the Dino-soarer's docking bay, locked inside a reinforced cage, was Goldenclaw. His hands and feet were manacled and he had a metal muzzle strapped over his jaws. His gaze was fixed upon Shady Lady, who was handcuffed to a passenger seat a few feet from the cage.

"The ogling is odious ... but I do find you fascinatingly fiendish," Shady Lady said in a whisper. Goldenclaw glanced down, embarrassed, and a smile flashed across Shady Lady's face. "Spynosaur says you're dangerous ... destined for diabolical deeds."

"You were right about me, Lady. You said I was decent, deep down ... and I was, once. But I've changed," Goldenclaw explained. "If only I had another chance, I could prove it to you ... but it's too late."

"Not necessarily. As I said to Spynosaur, I'm a dab hand at disentanglement," Shady Lady whispered. With a *K-KLiNK* the handcuffs that tethered her to her chair sprang open. She slunk out of her chair and slid across the docking bay as silently as a shadow to Goldenclaw's cage. Then, from her dress, she produced Goldenclaw's golden control pad. "I'm also a thorough thief – I pinched *this* from the meddling mole, even as he chained me to that chair."

"Lady, you never cease to amaze me..." said Goldenclaw, a grin spreading across his face.

Meanwhile in the cockpit, Holey Moley sat on the dashboard, peering out of the window. Amber stared at him. Finally she took a deep breath.

"Moley ... I'm sorry I accused you of being a mole. I mean, *the* mole," she said.

"That's all right," replied Holey Moley. "To be honest, it's been nice to actually help for once."

"But if you're not the mole, who is?" Amber mused.

"I bet it was Red Herring all along!" cried Danger Monkey from the pilot's seat. "I'll crack 'er fishbowl! I'll leave 'er out in the sun! I'll replace 'er fish-food with an inferior product!"

Spynosaur reached into a pocket in his spy-suit and took out the chunk of spytanium. He held it up, its distinct red glow illuminating his face.

"Only the mole knows for certain who the mole is," he said. "Even Goldenclaw might not know their true identity, or—"

The chunk of spytanuim suddenly flew out of Spynosaur's hand! It streaked past Amber's head, through the air into the docking bay. Everyone spun round to see Goldenclaw and Shady Lady, free of their shackles and at the controls of the Ray Emitter, the spytanuim caught in its Gravity Ray.

"Give that back!" growled Amber, jumping up as Goldenclaw plucked the spytanium from the air and shoved it down his pants. Spynosaur leaped out of his seat and raced towards the docking bay but Goldenclaw was even faster. He grabbed the Ray Emitter in both arms and hauled it over his head.

"I'm finished with this – you can have it!" he cried. He flung the machine at Spynosaur and sent him careening backwards into the cockpit controls.

"Sorry, Spynosaur, I'm not prepared to putrefy in prison!" said Shady Lady, her hand hovering over the docking bay release lever on the wall. "And Goldenclaw has promised a plan that is deeply diabolical!"

"Wait, don't—!" began Spynosaur, but with a CLUNK! and a WHIRRR, Shady Lady opened the docking bay – and she and Goldenclaw were sucked out into the air.

By the time Danger Monkey had closed the docking bay and dropped the Dino-soarer to sea level, Goldenclaw and Shady Lady were nowhere to be found. Even the Dino-soarer's scanners couldn't find them – it was as though they'd disappeared.

"And they stole the control pad that I stole!" cried Holey Moley. "It was right here, in my back pocket. I probably should have noticed it was missing since it's three times my size..."

"No doubt Goldenclaw used the control pad to summon his Gold Rush wave to collect him from the ocean below," Spynosaur mused. "It's carried them off to who knows where."

"I'll file 'is nails! I'll floss 'is teeth! I'll lance 'is ear wax!" growled Danger Monkey. "Except we ain't got the slightest clue where 'e's gone or what 'e's plannin'."

"Wait, that reminds me!" cried Holey Moley, producing a folded piece of golden paper out of his spy-suit. "When I was hiding in Goldenclaw's underpants, I came across this, tucked in between his ... you know."

"Eww," groaned Amber as Holey Moley handed the paper to Spynosaur. Upon it was written:

Spynosaur unrolled it and inspected it closely. Amber saw the colour drain from her dad's scaly cheeks.

"We have to get back to headquarters, and fast," said Spynosaur grimly. "The world is in terrible danger and the only way to save it is to dig the mole out of its hole."

# 20.
# THE TRUTH, THE MOLE TRUTH, AND NOTHING BUT THE TRUTH

SATURDAY 18:04

DEPARTMENT 6
HEADQUARTERS, LONDON.
AGAIN.

The Dino-soarer returned Spynosaur and company to Department 6 headquarters at supersonic speed. Spynosaur burst into the control room carrying the Ray Emitter aloft, closely followed by Amber, Danger Monkey and Holey Moley.

"The Variable Super Science Ray Beam Emitter! You found it!" squealed Dr Newfangle, throwing his arms round his invention even before Spynosaur had deposited it on the floor. "You poor thing!

Lost out there in the big, wide world, not knowing where you were, everyone turning your dial this way and that ... you must have been so scared!"

"Danger Monkey, make sure all of Goldenclaw's henchimals are rounded up," Spynosaur commanded. "Holey Moley, we need to make sure no one can ever break into Department 6 again. As Head of Security, I know you're up to the job."

"Really? I mean, absolutely! I can help with— I mean, I can do that!" Holey Moley cried, scurrying away happily. "Head of Security, coming through!"

"And what about us, Dad? What are we going to do?" asked Amber.

"*I'll* tell you what you're going to do – you're going to stand in my office while I shout at you until my face turns red!" bellowed M11 from her office at the other end of the room.

For once, Spynosaur did not reply – he strode silently into M11's office (with Amber hot on his heels) and closed the door.

"Blast it to smithereens, there's one thing being a reckless maverick, but quite another being utterly incompetent!" continued M11, barely pausing for breath. "Not only do you disappear for days without so much as a phone call, but when you finally re-emerge – when you *finally* have a chance to apprehend Shady Lady and her monstrous new partner-in-crime – you let her get away! Well, enough's enough! Hand over your gadgets and personalized Department 6 stationery – as far as I'm concerned, you're finished here!"

"Three days ago, I would have happily obeyed," Spynosaur replied. "But I've got my groove back ... and I have a mission to accomplish. Speaking of which, any luck finding the Department mole?"

"Since you ask, no," huffed M11. "I have my suspicions about Red Herring, but—"

"*But*," Spynosaur interrupted firmly. "While Red Herring or even Holey Moley could have told Goldentoe the location of the Vault or turned off the alarm, only you and I knew about the location of the spytanium in Tibet."

"Are – are you trying to tell me *you're* the mole?" snapped M11.

"No, M11," Spynosaur replied. "You are."

"Wait, what?" said Amber.

"What are you suggesting, agent?" M11 snarled, her moustache twitching wildly. "That I planned all this from the start? That I discovered Goldentoe's infatuation with Shady Lady and convinced him to employ an army of henchmen and create an arsenal of weaponry just to impress her? That I had him create a fake security firm and told him when, where and how to spring Shady Lady from incarceration? That I gave him the precise location of Ronald Ray-Gun within the Vault and, while wearing a sly-spy *stealth-suit*, turned off the alarm without anyone noticing so he could steal it? That I even told Goldentoe the secret location of the spytanium? That I did all this in the slim hope of creating you a new arch-enemy, because I thought you were losing the will to spy?"

"Exactly," replied Spynosaur. "Also, you're wearing a badge that says I'M THE MOLE on it."

M11 looked down at the large badge pinned to her lapel. Her moustache twitched and she let out a long sigh.

"Perhaps, on some level, I wanted to be found out," she said at last, unpinning the badge and tossing it on to her desk.

"Wait, you *are* the mole?" Amber shrieked.

"Yes, I'm the mole!" M11 snapped. "I betrayed everyone in the Department and put countless lives in danger! But in my defence, I was only trying to help."

"Trying to help? Goldenclaw nearly killed my dad!" Amber cried.

"I didn't even know there *was* a Goldenclaw! Goldentoe and I communicated by text – and occasionally carrier pigeon – so I had no idea he'd been transformed into that *thing* until today! I mean, transforming himself into a monstrous half-man, half-dinosaur? How could he possibly have come up with such an insane idea?"

"Well, uh, I … that's not the point!" Amber snapped. "Tell her, Dad! Tell her it's all her fault!"

"What was I supposed to do?" M11 boomed. "You saw what Spynosaur was like – since he ran out of proper villains, he went off the boil! The half-hearted spying, the lack of explosions ... blast it to smithereens, the poetry! It was as if he—"

"Didn't want to be a spy any more," interrupted Amber. "I didn't think anyone else had noticed."

"Of course I noticed!" cried M11, her moustache quivering. "The sorry truth of the matter is that Spynosaur is the only decent agent in Department 6. If he decided to call it a day, what then? We'd be shut down in no time! I'd be out of a job! I can't face retirement ... I can't face coffee mornings and book groups and not being able to shout at whoever I please!" She took a deep breath, smoothed her moustache and turned to Spynosaur.

"But more importantly, if you gave up, who would save the world when the next *real* villain comes along? The world needs you, agent. The world needs Spynosaur."

"Well, I can't argue with that," Spynosaur said. Then he folded his arms, eyeballing M11 and Amber in turn. "Look, I know you both meant well, and I'm flattered that you went to all this effort, but you've behaved *very* badly. I need you to promise – both of you – never to try and create me a nemesis, ever again."

"We promise," said Amber and M11 sheepishly.

"Good. And I promise *you*, I'm a spy, from nose to tail," Spynosaur added, pressing his fists against his hips. "I'll always be ready to defend the defenceless ... I'll always do battle with the forces of evil ... I will always be there if the world needs saving! Which reminds me, the world needs saving."

Spynosaur handed M11 Goldenclaw's plans. She unfolded the piece of golden paper and peered at it.

"Is ... is that what I think it is?" she uttered in horror, the colour draining from her moustache. "He has the spytanium! Surely he can't be planning to— Blast it to smithereens!"

"Exactly," Spynosaur said. "Rather *poetic*, don't you think?"

"Da-ad, no poems – you promised," groaned Amber.

"What I mean is, Goldenclaw is embracing his inner dinosaur," Spynosaur replied. "So, M11, any idea where Goldenclaw might carry out his diabolical plan?"

"Ah, well, I *might* have given him the coordinates for an abandoned oil rig in the middle of the North Sea ... but I thought he was just going to use it as a holiday home!" confessed M11. "It appears

I've abandoned the rule book *and* doomed the entire world. This isn't going to go down well at the Annual General Meeting..."

"You're secret is safe with us, M11 – Amber and I will handle things off the record," said Spynosaur. He turned to his sidekick and gave her a wink. "Ready for a rematch?"

# 21.
# THE SUPER RAY EMITTER
## AKA RONALD RAY-GUN 2.0

AN ABANDONED OIL RIG
IN THE NORTH SEA.
NOT BEING USED AS A HOLIDAY HOME

A storm was brewing. Rain lashed the oil rig and the churning ocean weaved around its four vast, steel legs. In the middle of the rig's central platform, covered in a golden tarpaulin, was a mysterious structure as large as a house.

A golden wave suddenly swirled out of the ocean, curving upwards in a conical shape to the rig's main platform and depositing its passengers, Goldenclaw and Shady Lady, on to the deck.

"That ... was notably nauseating," said Shady Lady, dizzied and dazed from hours of being conveyed through the ocean.

"My apologies for the unusual method of transportation," said Goldenclaw as the Gold Rush wave retreated into the ocean. "But everything has been leading to this moment. Behold!"

He strode over to the covered structure and tore down the tarpaulin to reveal a Ray Emitter of epic proportions. It was ten times bigger than Dr Newfangle's machine and painted from top to bottom in twenty-four carat gold.

"You had your own Ray Emitter built?" Shady Lady said, the great machine towering over her.

"I call it the *Super* Ray Emitter! Ronald Ray-Gun 2.0!" Goldenclaw exclaimed. "Retro-engineered from Department 6's model ... but vastly improved. So basically loads bigger." He placed the spytanium in the Super Ray Emitter's power core. The monolithic machine rumbled with raw power. "What do you think? It cost me a fortune..."

"I'm impressed," Shady Lady remarked, giddy with the possibilities. "You're definitely dangerous! With this contraption we can conquer countries and crush our competitors!"

"We could ... but I have something even better in mind," he replied, humming happily as he turned the Science Dial to GRAVITY RAY. A moment later, a bright, white beam streaked upwards from the Super Ray Emitter, lighting up the night sky, before disappearing into space. "You see, taking over the world is all well and good," added Goldenclaw, "but *destroying* it is even better."

"Did you say, 'destroying'?" asked Shady Lady.

"When I was transformed, I realized that there was only one way to prove myself to you," Goldenclaw continued. "Even now, the Super Ray Emitter has locked on to a passing meteor, far off in space ... a meteor that is being pulled here faster than the speed of possibility! When it crashes, the impact will bring about a new Ice Age! It will wipe out all human life, just as a meteor wiped out the dinosaurs, hundreds of millions of years ago! Poetic, isn't it?"

"I desire danger, not *death*, you mutated maniac!" Shady Lady protested, making a dash for the Super Ray Emitter. "Shut off your mad machine, or I will!"

"No!" boomed Goldenclaw, leaping in front of her. He swept up the abandoned tarpaulin, and cast it like a net over Shady Lady. He bundled her up inside it, knotted it tightly and slung her over his shoulder. "I'm sorry but not even you can escape our *destiny*," he added as Shady Lady howled in protest. "By destroying the world, we'll be together forever, immortalized in infamy! We'll be the ultimate power couple! Admittedly we'll be dead since the world will be destroyed but—"

"Goldenclaw!"

Goldenclaw glanced upwards to see the Dino-soarer materializing in the sky above the oil rig. The docking bay opened and Spynosaur leaped out, landing with a **KRONNG!** a few metres from the Super Ray Emitter.

"You're too late this time, Spynosaur!" Goldenclaw boomed. "The world is doomed!"

"Yes, I understand the *gravity* of the situation," Spynosaur replied, staring up at the ray as it sliced a path into space. He took a moment to strike a battle-ready pose. "I've seen your plans,

Goldenclaw. Do you really think plunging the Earth into a new Ice Age will warm the heart of Shady Lady? Just turn it off and let's get to the real business of me stylishly defeating you."

"I crushed you last time we fought — even your mightiest blow couldn't keep me down," said Goldenclaw, gently placing the bundled-up Shady Lady on to the deck. "What makes you think you stand a chance against me now?"

"You may have been made to be my perfect nemesis, Goldenclaw," replied Spynosaur. "But you've only been doing this for three days — I've been spectacularly impressive for a *lifetime*."

"You can't stop the inevitable!" Goldenclaw roared. "In two minutes, the meteor will strike the Earth!"

"That's convenient," Spynosaur said, checking his Super Secret Spy Watch™, "because I only need one minute and fifty-nine seconds to defeat you."

01:58

THIS IS THE CLIMACTIC PART, WHERE GOOD AND EVIL FIGHT

01:30

THE VILLAIN THINKS HE'LL WIN THE DAY, BUT LET'S HOPE HE'S NOT RIGHT

01:02

00:51

SPYNOSAUR MUST PROVE
THAT HE'S A HERO WITHOUT EQUAL

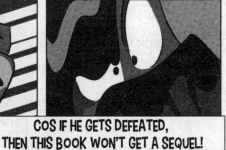

COS IF HE GETS DEFEATED,
THEN THIS BOOK WON'T GET A SEQUEL!

SPYNOSAUR!

Goldenclaw stumbled back, reeling from Spynosaur's attack. He wobbled on his feet, before crumpling to the ground.

"I don't ... want to say ... I told you so," Spynosaur panted. "No, wait, that's exactly what I want. Told you so!"

## 00:07

"Even if you win ... you've lost," groaned Goldenclaw, managing to point a claw into the air. "Time's up – look!"

Spynosaur glanced upwards. A huge, granite-black meteor had appeared in the night sky. It was so vast and close that it blocked out the stars as it sped towards them.

## 00:04

"Oh, yes, that," said Spynosaur coolly. He checked his Super Secret Spy Watch™ again. "Amber, would you do the honours?"

"On it!" came a cry. The air next to the Super Ray Emitter shimmered, and the almost-invisible Amber appeared. She wasted no time in reaching for the emitter's Science Dial. "One Reduction Ray, coming up!"

## 00:03

"Reduction Ray? But— No!" Goldenclaw roared as the Super Ray Emitter's white beam turned a bright blue. The Reduction Ray bombarded the meteor with the unlimited energies of the spytanium. In moments, it had shrunk so fast it almost seemed to disappear from the sky. Until:

PLUNK!

"NO!" howled Goldenclaw again, as the meteor landed harmlessly on the platform and bounced to a halt at Spynosaur's feet. It was no bigger than a tennis ball.

"I told you, I saw your secret plan," said Spynosaur, plucking the still-smoking meteor from the ground. "You may have built a bigger Ray Emitter but in all other ways it duplicated the Ronald Ray-Gun exactly – including *all* of its remarkable functions."

"You gave us the problem and the solution, *Goldendope*!" added Amber, waving Goldenclaw's secret plan around.

"Spynosaur, my saviour!" cried Shady Lady's muffled voice from inside the tarpaulin. "I knew you'd know how to foil this foul fiend! I was plainly playing along, a devious deception to dupe—"

"Save the alliteration for your *P.O.I.S.O.N.-ous* partners in crime," said Spynosaur. "You'll have plenty to talk about back in prison."

"SPYNOSAUR!" yelled Goldenclaw. He reached into his pants and took out his control pad. A moment later, the Gold Rush wave burst out of the ocean, swirling over the top of the platform and waiting for Goldenclaw's next command...

"Catch!" cried Spynosaur. He flung the shrunken meteor at Goldenclaw, smashing his control pad into pieces. Without a command, the hundreds of gallons of robotic nano-wave crashed on top of its master – and swept him over the platform into the ocean below. Within seconds, Goldenclaw was swallowed into the dark, churning waters.

"Should we go after him?" said Amber, racing to the edge of the oil rig.

"We'll get Red Herring to have a look for him ... eventually," Spynosaur replied, retrieving the spytanium from inside the Super Ray Emitter.

Then he picked up the bundled Shady Lady and flung her over his shoulder.

"You saurian sadist! Free me forthwith!" hissed Shady Lady.

Spynosaur gave Amber a wink. Then he tapped his Super Secret Spy Watch™ and the Dino-soarer descended on to the platform.

"So now what?" asked Amber as they climbed on board. "Back to headquarters or..."

"I think you're forgetting the most important part of any mission," Spynosaur replied, guiding the Dino-soarer into the air. "We *always* blow something up. Care to do the honours?"

"Finally!" Amber cried and trained the Dino-soarer's missile launchers on the Super Ray Emitter.

HE'S THE SPY THAT SURPRISES!
HE'S THE AGENT WHO'LL AMAZE!
FIGHTING FOR RIGHT,
THANKS TO THOSE SUPER SCIENCE RAYS.
HE FACED A MIGHTY ENEMY
AND PUT HIM IN HIS PLACE.
HE OUTWITTED HIS NEMESIS,
THEN PUNCHED HIM IN THE FACE!

# SPYNOSAUR!

SO IF YOU NEED A HERO
WHO'S A CUT ABOVE THE REST,
THEN DO THE SAME AS GOLDENCLAW
AND PUT HIM TO THE TEST.
AMBER AND HER FATHER
ARE ON HAND TO SAVE THE DAY,
AND BLOW STUFF UP TO SMITHEREENS
IF IT GETS IN THEIR WAY!

# SPYNOSAUR!
# SPYNOSAUUUUUR!

# EPILOGUE

 THE HIGHLANDS OF IRELAND

With the world safe once more, Spynosaur and Amber dropped Shady Lady off at Department 6 headquarters, before paying a visit to what was left of Trouserfall Lodge. The wreck of the house lay in the middle of a large field a few miles from its original spot. They found Grandma Gambit there, stirring a cracked pot filled with soup on a broken stove in what was left of the kitchen.

"Sure, I wondered where you two had got to," said Grandma. "And for a while, who you were."

"Sorry about your house, Great-Grandma," said Amber.

"House? What house?" asked Grandma Gambit, looking around. "I think it's plain to see I'm the outdoorsy type."

"Don't worry, Grandma, we'll rebuild Trouserfall even better than before," said Spynosaur. "But first I need to ask you a favour."

"You should know better than to ask me anything," said Grandma Gambit. "I'll have forgotten the question before you've finished asking it."

"That's what I'm counting on," Spynosaur replied, producing the chunk of spytanium from his spy-suit. "This element holds so much power that no one can be trusted with it ... even the head of Department 6. I need to make sure it stays hidden."

"Leave it with me – I'll have forgotten where I've put it by teatime," Grandma Gambit replied, taking the spytanuim. "Now, will you not stay for some soup?"

"Actually, Amber here is overdue a plate of her mum's Scrambled Egg Surprise," replied Spynosaur, giving his grandmother a peck on the cheek. "I'd better get her home."

Grandma Gambit watched as Spynosaur and Amber climbed aboard the Dino-soarer and took to the air. After a moment she looked at the chunk of spytanium in her hand.

"Sure, what's this now?" she said. Then she shrugged and dropped it into the pot.

As Spynosaur piloted the Dino-soarer back to Little Wallop, Amber stared out of the cockpit, into the dawn sky. After a while she said, "Are you *sure* you're not going to give up spying, Dad? I mean, I get to go home and eat eggs, but you... Don't you ever think about having a normal life?"

Spynosaur smiled a wide, toothy smile.

"Battling evil, vanquishing villainy, being incredibly impressive — that is normal life," he replied. "Anything else would feel very odd indeed, don't you think?"

"*Definitely*," said Amber, and gave her dad a hug. "It's just a shame I only get to see you when the world needs saving."

"Oh, I'm sure the world will need saving again before long," said Spynosaur.

"Hope it's not *too* long," replied Amber.

Her dad smiled. "So do I," he said.

# BONUS PUBLIC SERVICE ANNOUNCEMENT!

It was a Tuesday and the leaders of the free world were having a get-together at World Leader Headquarters. Suddenly their HQ came under attack from the revolutionary robot, A.N.N.A.K.I.S.T. and her cyborg henchmen, the Free Radicals.

Fortunately Spynosaur and Amber appeared just in time. With Spynosaur's improbably impressive spy skills and Amber's ninja stuff, they made short work of the robotic rebels.

"I'd say we tested their mettle," said Spynosaur, smashing the last of the robots with his tail.

"Da-ad," groaned Amber.

"Thanks, Spynosaur!" cried the leaders of the free world.

"You're welcome … and keep up the good work," Spynosaur replied. "But remember, criminals, evil robots, zombie barbershop quartets and danger are everywhere, so if you see anything suspicious, be sure to alert the authorities."

"Or your nearest dinosaur super-spy-and-sidekick super team!" added Amber.

"Also, never go swimming in a thunderstorm, and don't eat cheese after six p.m.," concluded Spynosaur.

"Well, until next time!"

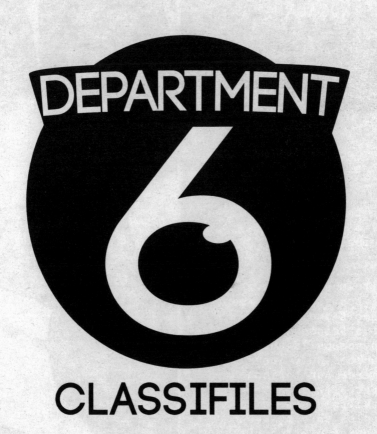

# DEPARTMENT 6

# CLASSIFILES

CODE NAME:
## SPYNOSAUR

AKA:
Agent Gambit, A47

Primary Spy-ciality:
Advanced Spying

Secondary Spy-ciality:
Puns

Motto:
"I'm going to make crime extinct."

With the brainwaves of top super-spy Agent Gambit and the body of a Deinonychus, Spynosaur is the world's only Super Secret Agent Dinosaur! Specializes in stylishly saving the world, defying death and infuriating his boss, M11. Spynosaur is an expert combatant, a cunning detective and a master of disguise ... as long as no one spots his tail.

DEPARTMENT
6

CODE NAME:
## AMBER

AKA: Amber Gambit,
"Dad's Little Poppet"

Primary Spy-ciality:
Ninja stuff

Secondary Spy-ciality:
Spy stuff

Motto:

"LAUGHING KANGAROO
WAGON WHEEL THWACK
ATTACK!"

Spynosaur's daughter
and sidekick, Amber
Gambit is as dedicated
as her dad to fighting
crime and foiling
fiends wherever they
find them. Highly
resourceful and
skilled, with more
ninja moves than you
can shake a foot at,
Amber Gambit keeps her
double life and ninja
skills secret - even
from her mum.

DEPARTMENT
6

CODE NAME:
AGENT GAMBIT
⟦REDACTED⟧

⟦REDACTED⟧

CODE NAME:
# MRS GAMBIT
Amber's mum.

DON'T TELL HER ANYTHING.

DEPARTMENT
6